When I reached the edge of the Dog Bowl I looked down. Rufus was sitting beside a guy around my age, who was holding the end of his leash and patting him on the head.

"Sounds like you're in trouble, buddy," the guy said to Rufus. He had a really nice, calming voice. The boy, I mean, not Rufus. He turned and handed me the leash. For a second, our hands touched.

"Thanks for catching him," I said.

"No problem." He looked at me and smiled, and that's when I noticed his eyes. They were dark brown, just like Rufus's. His hair was a dark golden-brown, and it fell in his face a little bit. *He's kind of cute,* I thought.

XOXOXOX

Read all the FIRST KISSES books:

FIRST KISSES

Puppy Love

Jenny Collins

HARPER TEEN

An Imprint of HarperCollins*Publishers*

This book is for Roger.

Chapter One

It was Rufus who started all the trouble.

Wait. That's not fair. Rufus was just chasing the squirrel. So I guess you could say it was the squirrel's fault. But that's not really right either. The squirrel was minding its own business until Rufus decided to chase it. And I can't blame a squirrel for what happened. I mean, it was only doing what squirrels do. But then Rufus was only doing what dogs do, so now we're back where we started.

I should back up. My name is Allie. Actually,

it's Allison Elizabeth Morris, but no one calls me that except for my great-grandmother Codwell (my mom's mom's mom) and she's something like eleventy-nine years old and lives in a house filled with way too many doilies and way too many cats. Not that she isn't great. She is. I love visiting her. Well, except for the doilies. They kind of freak me out. And the cats. I'm not really a cat person. I like dogs.

I don't just like dogs; I *love* dogs. In fact, I think dogs are just about the greatest things ever invented. I know, the rule is supposed to be that girls like cats and guys like dogs. But that's just dumb. Don't get me wrong. Cats are okay. I think they're cute, and I don't mind when they sit on me or want to be petted. But dogs are something else. Dogs are like people, but better. Not that I'm antisocial or anything. I like people. It's just that dogs are, I don't know, more reliable maybe. You always know where you stand with a dog. With people, sometimes it's hard to tell.

Anyway, I'm almost fourteen, and I'm going

to be in ninth grade when school starts again. I'm pretty excited about that, but I'm not in a rush for summer to be over. I'm having too much fun with the dogs. Well, most of the dogs. There's one I could do without. Her *and* her owner. But I'm getting way ahead of myself again.

I'll start at the beginning. Not all the way back, like when I was born or anything, but right before what my friend Shan would call the Regrettable Incident with Rufus and the squirrel. See, my mother has this business called Perfect Paws. It's a dog grooming salon. She started it when I was little, so I grew up around dogs. When I was really small, my mom says I used to think I was a puppy. My first word wasn't *mama* or *dada*, it was *woof*. I'm serious!

I've been helping out at Perfect Paws since I was about eight or nine, washing the dogs and sweeping up hair—that kind of thing. But this year I wanted to do something more. A few months ago, I heard one of our customers talking about how she was sending her two kids to theater camp during the day so that they had something to do all summer. She joked that it would be nice if her Lhasa apso had somewhere to go too, so that he wasn't home alone all the time. Well, that got me thinking, and that night at dinner I suggested that we think about offering day care at Perfect Paws. My parents thought it was a pretty good idea, and we decided to try it over the summer and see what happened. Best of all, my mother put me in charge of it.

I really pushed the doggy day care idea to our customers, and the weekend before opening day we already had six sign-ups. I was kind of nervous because I wanted everything to go perfectly, and I tend to worry a little too much. So I decided to take my dog, Rufus, to the park for a walk. That almost always calms me down.

It's hard not to be relaxed around Rufus. He's the happiest dog I know: a big, brown mutt who thinks everything in the world was made just for him. My father calls him a

Labragrizzly because he looks like a Labrador retriever crossed with a grizzly bear. We rescued him from a shelter about five years ago. When we walked by his cage he was sitting all alone in the corner, looking like he didn't know what he'd done wrong to be abandoned by the people he loved. As soon as I saw him I knew he had to come home with us.

He's been my best friend ever since. Well, one of my two best friends. My best human friend is Shan, who I mentioned before. Everyone thinks Shan is short for Shannon, but it's not. She's just Shan. Shan Chan. I know, it's totally unfortunate, right? She says one good reason for her to get married is that she can get a new last name. But then sometimes she says she's going to keep her own name when she gets married, so who knows. With Shan you can never tell.

Shan and I have been friends almost as long as Rufus and I have. She was going to help me with the doggy day care, but then her parents decided she was going to spend the summer in

San Francisco with her grandparents, and that changed everything. I was really bummed that Shan wouldn't be here to have fun with me.

So anyway, Rufus and I went to the park. I love walking with him. He's curious about everything, and he always acts as if it's the first time he's sniffed grass or heard birds or seen people on bicycles, even though he's almost ten and we go to the park just about every day. There's no way to be sad when you're walking Rufus, or any dog for that matter. They're just so happy to be outside that their happiness rubs off on you. I'm telling you, the way to get yourself feeling good again when you're sad isn't to eat a dozen chocolate chip cookies or buy some new shoes, it's to walk a dog.

And I *was* feeling better. Walking Rufus, I knew I'd be able to handle six dogs for a day. Yes, I still wished Shan could be there to do it with me, but I knew I would be okay. Six dogs isn't that many, and three of them were big. Contrary to popular belief, big dogs are a lot easier to handle than small dogs. Mostly they just like to play a little fetch and take naps. But the little ones stay active all day long. Personally, I think it's because little dogs have just as much energy as the big ones but it takes longer for them to use it up.

I was thinking of games I could play with the dogs when the squirrel made its entrance. I didn't even see it. But Rufus did. And if there's one thing Rufus can't resist, it's a squirrel. They make him crazy. And being a bear-dog, Rufus is really strong, so when he wants to run after something you have to be prepared for it, which I usually am. But for some reason my mind was somewhere else just then, so when the leash suddenly jerked me forward I ended up falling all over myself. There I was, lying on the grass, watching Rufus's leash drag along behind him while he ran away, barking his head off.

I got up as soon as I could and ran after him, calling his name, which I knew wasn't going to help. When Rufus is chasing a squirrel, he uses his whole brain to focus on catching it. You can yell all you want to, but he won't hear you. I yelled anyway, mainly so everyone watching me would think I was trying to do something to stop him.

You'd think the squirrel would go to the first tree it saw and climb it, right? Well, this one didn't. It just kept running, with Rufus behind it and me behind Rufus. I tried to keep up with them, but let's face it, four legs are always going to be faster than two.

They got farther and farther away from me until finally they reached the edge of what we call the Dog Bowl—this part of the park where there's a dip between some small hills. A lot of people bring their dogs there because it's a great place to toss balls and let the dogs run around together without them getting in the way of the rollerbladers, joggers, and people pushing strollers through the park.

Rufus and the squirrel disappeared over the edge of the Dog Bowl. Then I heard Rufus stop barking, which was weird. When he's after a squirrel he barks until you get him away from it. I don't know what I thought might have happened to Rufus, but I suddenly got scared. What if he was hurt? Or maybe the squirrel had friends. Lots of friends, like a little squirrel army. It's stupid, I know. I never said that I'm always rational, okay? I'm a worrier.

When I reached the edge of the Dog Bowl I looked down, half expecting to see Rufus surrounded by crazy warrior squirrels. Instead, he was sitting beside a guy who was holding the end of his leash and patting Rufus on the head. The guy was probably not much older than me, and my first thought was, great—it would be just my luck that he would end up being in my high school. He was looking around, and I could tell he was trying to figure out what moron let her dog run away. Being the moron in question, I walked down the hill toward him, trying to think of something to say so I wouldn't look as dumb as I felt.

When Rufus saw me, he looked up with his big brown eyes and started wagging his tail, which he always does when he knows he's done something bad. He knows it's hard to be angry at him when he looks like that. Usually it works. But I was pretty mad at him, so I tried to ignore his adorableness.

"Not this time, mister," I told him.

"Sounds like you're in trouble, buddy," the guy said to Rufus. He had a really nice, calming voice. The boy, I mean, not Rufus. He turned and handed me the leash. "I take it this isn't his first offense?" he said.

"He was on squirrel patrol," I answered, taking the leash. For a second, our hands touched.

The guy nodded. "You've got to watch out for those squirrels," he said, scratching Rufus behind the ears. "I hate to tell you this, but that's a losing battle."

I laughed. I couldn't tell if he was talking to me or Rufus. "Thanks for catching him," I said.

"No problem." He looked at me and smiled, and that's when I noticed his eyes. They were dark brown, just like Rufus's. His hair was a dark golden-brown, and it fell in his face a little bit. *He's kind of cute,* I thought. Then I realized I was staring at him, and I looked away. I didn't want him to think I was an incompetent dog walker *and* all into him.

"We've got to go," I said, tugging at Rufus so that he got up and followed me. "Thanks again."

I walked back up the hill. Part of me wanted to look back and see if the guy was watching me, but I just kept going. For some reason, if he wasn't watching me, I didn't want to know. So I kept my eyes on Rufus and walked until I couldn't see over the edge of the Dog Bowl. Then I breathed a sigh of relief.

"Thanks for making me look stupid," I told Rufus. "And you had to do it in front of the cutest guy you could find, didn't you?"

Rufus looked up at me and wagged his tail. This time I couldn't resist him. I knelt down, rubbed his ears, and kissed him on the nose. "I know," I said. "You can't help it."

He licked my face.

"Dog kisses," I said, giving him a hug. "The best kind."

I slipped my hand through the handle of his leash and wrapped it around my wrist. If any more squirrels crossed our path, I'd be ready for them. "Come on," I said to Rufus. "Let's go home."

Chapter Two

My first customers on Monday morning were the Twins. Their real names are Walter and Wendell, but everyone calls them the Twins because you can't tell them apart. They're pugs, and they live with old Mrs. Dibberson down the block. The Twins are super friendly, and having them come in first thing seemed like a good sign for the rest of the day. They were wagging their curly tails and snorting, the way pugs do when they're happy, and they kept tangling their leashes around Mrs. Dibberson's feet.

"Walter!" she said. "Wendell! Stop that at once." She looked at me and sighed. "I don't know why I bother," she said. "They never listen."

"I'm sure they'll behave," I told her. "Are you going to leave them all day?"

"Just until two," Mrs. Dibberson said as she tried to pull one foot out of the knot the Twins had made. "I'm having company over for lunch. Actually, it's not really company. It's Mr. Dibberson's aunt. She's frightfully dull. Worst of all, she despises dogs. Can you imagine?"

"No," I said as I helped her untangle herself. "Especially the Twins. Who couldn't love you?" I asked Walter and Wendell as they jumped up to lick my nose, grunting like little pigs.

"I'll miss them," Mrs. Dibberson said. "But I'm sure you'll take good care of them."

"I will," I assured her. "We're going to have a great day."

Mrs. Dibberson left, and I'd just put the Twins in the big backyard behind the store with Rufus, when the first of the big dogs arrived. Pythagoras is a Newfoundland, huge and black and furry. He came in with Mr. Wexman, who's going to be my math teacher this year. Mr. Wexman teaches summer school, so he'd arranged for Pythagoras to stay with us for a few hours every day. I especially wanted to impress him, since math is one of my favorite subjects and I'm hoping to do well in his class.

"Hey, Py," I said, patting the dog's huge head. "You ready for a day away from your dad?"

Py answered me by holding out one big paw. I took it and shook. Py responded by slobbering on my hand.

"Sorry," Mr. Wexman said.

"No problem," I told him, picking up a towel and wiping my slimy hand.

"I'll be back around two thirty," said Mr. Wexman. "Hopefully he won't drown anyone before then."

I introduced Py to Walter and Wendell (he's met Rufus a bunch of times, so they knew each other already) and watched the two pugs scamper around the big dog's feet. He didn't seem to mind, so I left them to get acquainted and went back inside to greet the next arrival. There were three other dogs scheduled for the day, and about five minutes later they all came in at once.

The last little dog was Princess Emmeline Merriweather Talbot. Emmy's name makes her sound fancy, but she's actually a mutt. We don't really know what she's a mix of, but she looks like a cross between a German shepherd and a collie, only shrunk down to about half the size of those dogs, so that what she really looks like is a big raccoon. My mother's friend Carter Talbot, who runs a catering company, found her hanging around his van one day after a wedding, trying to get at the leftover meatballs he'd put in the back. He took her home, and she's been coming in twice a month ever since for a shampoo and toenail clipping.

The two big dogs were Figaro and Skunk. Figaro's a Lab, like Rufus, only he's yellow instead of brown. He lives two streets over from us with this young couple, the Berds. Skunk has been coming in ever since he was a puppy. He belongs to Reverend Skelton. He's a mutt, part husky and part wolf. And he loves skunks. Hence the name. He's always getting sprayed, and he comes in at least once a month for a vinegar-and-tomato-juice bath to get rid of the latest skunk smell. But his fur is so thick that you can never get it all out, and no matter how many times we bathe him, he always has this faint skunky smell to him.

"Three weeks without an incident," Reverend Skelton told me. "I think that's a record for him. Hopefully he won't break it today."

With Emmy, Figaro, and Skunk added to the backyard, we were ready for our first day of doggy day care. I stood watching everyone, making sure they were all getting along, and was pleased that all the dogs seemed to like one another. Rufus and Figaro were already sharing a stick, each of them chewing on an end. Py had found a shady spot under a tree to sit in, and had managed to produce a long string of drool that had almost reached the ground. Skunk was sniffing around, followed closely by the Twins, whose noses were twitching excitedly as they tried to figure out what their new friend smelled like. And Emmy was chasing a bee that was trying to feed on the nasturtiums that covered one of the fences. *So far, so good,* I thought happily. I was going to spend the day with dogs I knew and liked. What better way to start my summer?

"Excuse me," someone yelled out. "Is anyone working here or what?"

I went inside to see who could be shouting like that. When I saw who it was, my stomach immediately knotted up.

"Megan," I said. "What are you doing here?"

I need to stop for a minute and explain why I was surprised, and not in a good way, to see her. Megan is Megan Fitzmartin. She's also known, at least to me and Shan, as Miss Perfection. That's because she thinks she is. Perfect, I mean. And she likes to remind you as often as possible of this supposed fact, usually while telling you exactly what's wrong with *you*. Depending on your point of view, she's either the queen or the terror of James Madison Middle School. That point of view is usually determined by whether you're a guy or a girl. There are girls who like Megan, or at least pretend to so that she'll let them be her friends, but mostly it's the guys who act like she's the best thing since the iPod.

I know this makes me sound like I'm jealous of Megan, but honestly, she's awful. I mean, she *is* pretty. She has long, blond hair and bright blue eyes and all of that typical pretty-girl stuff going on. It's just her insides that need work. My mother keeps telling me that things will be different when we're in high school this fall, and Megan is a freshman and just as new and socially unacceptable as the rest of us. But I don't know. Girls like Megan have a way of escaping the torture the rest of us mere mortals have to endure. I bet she'll be prom queen right off the bat.

It doesn't help that I've never really thought

of myself as pretty, at least not in the way that Megan is pretty. My hair is reddish-brown, and most of the time I wear it in a ponytail because I'm always running around doing something and I don't have a lot of time to spend standing in front of the mirror with a curling iron or blow-dryer. I have green eyes and pale skin that freckles almost instantly if I get any sun, and since I love being outdoors, I almost always have a scattering of tan-colored dots on my face.

Where Megan is downright skinny, I'm what my dad calls "athletic." What he means is that I'm sort of a tomboy. I like to play soccer, and I try to go running a couple of times a week. Oh, and I went through this growth spurt last year and grew something like three inches. At first, being taller than so many of the other girls (and even some of the boys) in my class made me feel awkward, but I'm used to it now. I confess, though, that I'm still kind of waiting for my chest to catch up with the rest of me. My mom swears it will happen any day now, and mostly I don't worry about it, but sometimes—like when I look at Megan—I feel a little behind in that department.

Anyway, when I saw that it was Megan standing in front of the counter, I immediately felt kind of inadequate. She was wearing this completely cute pink sweater over a white T-shirt, and her jeans fit her perfectly. I, in comparison, was wearing a pair of old shorts and a blue polo shirt with the Perfect Paws logo embroidered on it. Sure, I was dressed that way because I was working with dogs, but I couldn't help thinking that Megan looked way better.

I wasn't shocked that she was yelling like that. Megan thinks everyone else exists to do what she wants, and when you don't, she usually yells, as if maybe you just didn't hear her and she needs to repeat herself. Still, I couldn't understand why she was there at all. She'd never come into the shop before.

Then I saw that she was holding a poodle in her arms. Now, not to disparage poodles or anything. They get a bad rap, and I know there are a lot of nice ones. But this poodle just looked like trouble. First of all, she had on a sweater. It was pink, just like Megan's. Maybe there are dogs who need to wear sweaters, like sled dogs or dogs who work outside in places where it's cold. But in June, no dog needs to wear a sweater. And this poodle was clipped and primped and puffed so much she looked like one of those bushes they turn into animal shapes.

"This is Tallulah," Megan informed me. "I want to leave her here for the day."

"Are you in summer school?" I asked her, wondering why she might need to put her dog in day care.

Megan sneered at me. "No, I'm not in summer school," she said, rolling her eyes and doing a bad imitation of my voice. "I'm going to the mall."

"You want to leave your dog here while you go shopping?" I said, assuming she was joking.

"Yes," said Megan. "Is that a problem?"

Just looking at Tallulah, I could tell she was going to be a handful. The fact that she belonged to Megan only made it worse. But my mother and Megan's mother are actually friends (Mrs. Fitzmartin is nice, so Shan and I have this theory that somehow her real baby got mixed up with Megan at the hospital), and I knew my mom would be upset if I turned Megan away. Besides, as my dad always says, a customer is a customer.

"No," I told Megan. "That's no problem."

"Good," Megan said, thrusting Tallulah at me. "I'll be back at six. Bye."

She turned and walked out, not even bothering to say good-bye to Tallulah or tell me anything about her, like if she got along with other dogs or was allergic to grass or liked biscuits. I looked down at the little dog in my arms. "I guess one more won't hurt," I said. "Maybe you'll be lucky number seven."

Tallulah looked up at me and bared her teeth.

"Or maybe not," I said as I took her to the backyard.

I took Tallulah's sweater off so she wouldn't

overheat, then put her down. The other dogs ran over to see the new arrival. Walter and Wendell were the first ones to try and greet her. Tallulah bared her teeth again, then nipped at Wendell's ear. He yipped and ran away, followed by his brother. The other dogs pulled back and stared at Tallulah, who turned in a tight little circle, growling at everyone.

She was just getting warmed up. Over the next few hours, everybody got a nip from Tallulah at some point. She stole the other dogs' toys. She barked for no reason. She kept digging at the fence, getting herself all dirty and tearing up the grass. She wouldn't listen, and every time I tried to get near her, she growled and ran away. Finally I gave up on her and left her alone while I played with the rest of the dogs.

Apart from Tallulah, everything was going really well. I was enjoying my first day on the job, and I was pleased that the day care idea seemed to be working. My mother was happy too.

"I'm impressed with how you're handling all these dogs," she said when she came out to check on things right after lunch. "You really have a way with them."

"All of them except Tallulah," I told her.

"She'll get used to being here," my mother said. "Give her time."

The thing was, I didn't want her to get used to being there. I wanted her gone. One day with her was bad enough. The thought that Megan might actually bring her *back* was too horrible to even think about. I didn't tell my mom that, though. She was so happy, that I wanted her to think everything was perfect.

In the afternoon, after the Twins and Py went home, I thought maybe it would be nice to take everyone for a walk. The dogs all got excited when they saw the leashes. Except for Tallulah. She wouldn't come near me. She just barked and snapped and ran away whenever I got within five feet of her.

"Fine," I told her. "You can stay here all by yourself while the rest of us have a nice walk."

I figured that being alone would be good for her, sort of like a time-out you might give to a kid who's misbehaving. Maybe if she saw that being nasty wasn't getting her anywhere she would start being nicer.

With everyone else leashed up, I took four happy dogs for a walk. We walked about five blocks in each direction, making a square, and everybody sniffed and peed and did what dogs do on walks. It was a nice end to the day, and I was already looking forward to having more fun the next day.

When we got back to the shop, it took me a minute to realize that something wasn't right. Then I realized that Tallulah wasn't barking. Not only wasn't she barking, she wasn't doing anything. I looked all around the backyard, thinking maybe I just couldn't see her. Then I saw the hole. Tallulah had dug under the fence. And hanging from the bottom of the fence was her collar. It had gotten caught, and she'd slipped right out of it.

"Tallulah!" I called, trying to sound as if

nothing was wrong. My mother was working in the little office at the back of the store, and I didn't want her to hear me. "Here, Tallulah!"

I didn't really expect her to come, and she didn't. But I couldn't think of anything else to do. I didn't want to accept the truth, which was that she had clearly run away.

"Now what?" I asked out loud. I looked at the other dogs, as if they might know where Tallulah had gone. They just sniffed at the hole under the fence and turned away. Probably, I thought, they were happy to see her go.

I looked at my watch. It was just after four. Megan was coming at six. That gave me two hours to find Tallulah. I figured that since my mother apparently hadn't noticed Tallulah's absence yet, she must have run off right before we got back from the walk, which meant she probably hadn't gotten very far. But I couldn't just leave the other dogs to go look for her. Their owners would be coming for them soon. And I really didn't want to ask my mother to cover for me because then she'd know that I'd screwed up. I was just going to have to wait until the other dogs went home, then hope I had enough time to find Tallulah before Megan showed up.

Suddenly, my perfect first day had become a nightmare.

Chapter Three

Luckily for me everyone arrived to pick up their dogs in the next half hour. My mother, absorbed in her paperwork, hadn't noticed that Tallulah was missing, and left to do some grocery shopping for dinner. With everyone gone, that gave me an hour and a half to find Tallulah. The only problem was, I had no idea where to look for her. I knew that once she'd gotten under the fence she could have gone anywhere. Because she wouldn't come to me even if I got near her, I knew it was a waste of time to just go up and down the streets calling her name.

My only hope was that someone else had already found her and had somehow managed to get her to come to them. Even then I'd have to find whoever had her and get her back. Without her collar and tags, anyone finding her would have no idea who she belonged to, and they certainly wouldn't know to call Perfect Paws. I was going to have to knock on every door and ask if anyone had seen her or caught her. But there was no way I could get to so many houses. I was doomed.

Unless, I thought, *she's at the pound*. That was my only real chance. If someone had caught Tallulah, they might have taken her to the animal shelter. But they also might have kept her. People usually feel sorry for strays, and it was possible someone had found Tallulah, thought she was cute, and decided to take her in.

Then I reminded myself that this was Tallulah I was talking about. Sure, someone might think she was cute. But then she'd probably bite them or do something else to make herself totally unappealing. Then the pound would look like a great idea. For the first time,

I hoped Tallulah was being her nasty little self.

I put the CLOSED sign on the shop door and prayed that my mother wouldn't come back for anything and see it. I know it was irresponsible to leave the shop, but the way I saw it, I was quickly becoming the queen of irresponsible.

The shelter isn't too far from the shop, so getting there on my bike took me only about ten minutes. Now it was getting close to five. If Tallulah wasn't there, I was a goner. I left my bike outside and ran in.

"Can I help you?" a woman behind the counter asked.

"I'm looking for a lost dog," I said. "A poodle. She would have come in today."

"Strays are in kennel three," she told me. "If you go through that door and down the hall, you'll see it. There should be a volunteer there to help you."

"Thanks," I said, rushing toward the door.

I found kennel number three and pushed open the door. As soon as I walked in, all the dogs started barking. A sad-looking boxer ran up to the door of his cage and looked at me hopefully, like maybe I was his missing owner. When he saw that I wasn't, he whined.

"I'm sorry, sweetie," I said, sticking my hand through the bars and rubbing his head. "I'm sure someone will be here for you soon."

"You shouldn't do that," a voice said, startling me.

I pulled my hand back. "Sorry," I said, turning around. "He just looked so sad."

When I saw who had spoken, I stopped talking. It took me a moment to realize that it was the guy from the park, the one who had helped me catch Rufus. The cute guy. He was wearing dirty coveralls with the shelter logo on the pocket, which is why I didn't recognize him at first. But even in dirty clothes he was still really cute.

"Oh," I said. "It's you."

"Do I know you?" he asked me.

"Yesterday," I said. "The park. You caught my dog for me."

"That's where I've seen you," he said. "I thought you looked familiar. Don't tell me you lost him again?"

"What?" I said, thinking about the way his eyes looked when he smiled at me. Then I remembered why I was there. "Oh. No. I'm not here for Rufus," I explained. "I'm looking for another dog."

"You lost another dog?" he said, looking shocked. "Is this, like, something you do on a regular basis?"

I felt myself blushing. "No," I said. "This one isn't mine. She belongs to a, uh, friend," I added. I didn't add that even though Tallulah wasn't mine, I *was* still the one who had lost her.

"What kind of dog?" the guy asked.

"A poodle," I said. "White. Small. Kind of snippy."

"You may be in luck," he said. "Someone brought in a poodle about an hour ago. He said she was digging up his flowers."

"That sounds like Tallulah," I said.

"Over here," he said, walking around the corner.

I followed him. He pointed to one of the cages. When I saw Tallulah sitting inside, I almost yelled with joy. "That's her!"

Tallulah looked at me and bared her teeth.

"She doesn't look too thrilled to see you," the guy said.

"She and I don't exactly get along," I told him. "I'm just doing this as a favor for my friend. I'm so glad she's here. Come on, Tallulah."

I knelt in front of the cage and patted my leg. Tallulah turned away from me and started licking her foot.

"Tallulah," I said, more firmly this time. She ignored me.

"Let me try," the guy suggested. He knelt beside me and whistled softly. "Tallulah," he said. "Come here, pretty girl."

Tallulah turned around and looked at him. She wagged her tail and trotted to the door. Sticking her nose out, she licked the guy's fingers gently.

"You just have to know how to talk to them," he told me.

I didn't say anything, but I could feel my cheeks heating up. I was annoyed that Tallulah was acting like a good dog for him. And, yes, I was also a tiny bit jealous that he had called her a pretty girl. I'll admit it. It may sound silly, but I kind of thought it would be nice if he called *me* pretty.

"I should get you home," I told Tallulah. "Your mommy will be missing you."

"That might be a problem," the guy told me.

"Problem?" I said. "Why?"

"Well, we're only supposed to let the dogs go home with their owners. You're not her owner."

"Oh, but I might as well be," I said. "Her owner is practically my best friend." I'm not used to lying, and I could tell my face was getting even redder, if that was possible.

"Yeah," he said. "But I could get in a lot of trouble."

"Please," I said, trying to sound sad. "I have her tags! And I can't stand to see her locked up in there. And I know her mom won't be able to come right away. Can't you just let me take her?"

He looked at Tallulah. "I don't know," he said. "I just started here. I'd hate to make a bad impression so soon."

35

I know exactly how you feel, I thought to myself. Only my bad impression was going to be made on Megan, and she would never let me forget it. I had to get Tallulah, and soon. I only had twenty minutes before Megan was coming to pick up her dog.

"I know it's sort of against the rules," I said, trying to look sad and helpless. "But she's so scared. Can't you help her?" *And me,* I thought, hoping he would give in.

He sighed. "Okay," he said. "But you can't say anything to anyone."

"Promise," I said. "Thank you so much."

He opened Tallulah's cage and picked her up. When he handed her to me, she looked at me and growled. I ignored her.

"Thanks again," I said. "I really, really appreciate it."

I left as quickly as I could without running. I had to get home, and fast. I was on my bike, holding Tallulah against my stomach with one hand and steering with the other, when I realized that, once again, I'd forgotten to get the cute guy's name. But I didn't have time to worry about that. I had to get back in time to meet Megan.

I made it with only a couple of minutes to spare. I was just putting Tallulah's sweater on her and trying to brush off as much of the dirt as I could when Megan came bursting through the door.

"What happened to her?" she shouted.

"Oh, she was just playing in the dirt," I said, trying to sound casual. "It's no big deal."

"No big deal?" Megan said. "Then why did I get a call from the animal shelter saying someone found my dog wandering around the streets?"

"You did?" I asked, hoping I sounded as confused as I was. How could anyone have phoned Megan? I hadn't told anyone at the shelter that Tallulah belonged to her. "You're sure?"

"Of course I'm sure, you idiot," Megan said. She snatched Tallulah from me. "I came here to find out what they were talking about."

"Maybe it was a mistake," I suggested. "As you can see, she's right here."

"Well, she wasn't right here when I got the call," Megan snapped. "I don't know how you got her back, but I know you managed to lose her somehow."

"She's fine," I pointed out. "A little dirty, but fine."

"That's not the point," said Megan. "The point is, you lost her. What kind of day care is this?"

"Megan, I'm sorry," I said.

"You should be," she said. "And you're going to be even sorrier when I tell everyone I know not to bring their dogs here. And don't think I'm paying you for today, either."

"No," I said. "Of course not." I was angry, and there were a few other things I wanted to say to her. But she was right. I hate to say it, but she was. I should never have left Tallulah alone. I was lucky that I'd found her at all.

"I should have known better than to trust you with her," said Megan, giving me one last evil look before storming out.

I closed my eyes and sighed. How had Megan found out about Tallulah being lost?

Unfortunately, the only answer to that question was the one answer I didn't want to believe — the cute guy must have called her. But why? And how did he know who Tallulah belonged to? I didn't know. And, really, it didn't matter. The damage was already done. I knew Megan would make good on her promise to tell everyone how I'd messed up. No one would want to bring their dogs to the girl who let them run away. It was only my first day, and already I'd run the business into the ground.

At least my mother wasn't around to see what had happened. That was the only good thing.

As I walked home with Rufus — we live only a few streets away from the shop — I went over and over in my head what had happened during the day. Megan was right; I was an idiot. And now everybody would think so.

And it was all that guy's fault. What a jerk. *Why did he have to call Megan?* I wondered. Didn't he trust me? Did he think I was trying to steal Tallulah or something? And how did he know she belonged to Megan? He probably thought I was completely incompetent. And I was an even bigger loser for thinking he was cute in the first place. Now, thanks to him, my perfect summer was ruined.

Chapter Four

The more I thought about it, the more frustrated I got. Sure, Tallulah was my responsibility, and because I wasn't watching her as closely as I should have been, she got out. But when I found her she was fine. It was an accident. But the guy at the pound apparently thought I needed to be punished. Why else would he have called Megan when he knew Tallulah was with me and was okay?

What a jerkboy. *Jerkboy* is a Shanword. That's the term my father came up with for Shan's weird way of describing things. She's really good at creating them, and sometimes she comes up with Shanwords that are totally on target.

I decided to call the guy Jerkboy whenever I thought about him. Not that I was thinking about him, or his big, brown eyes, or the way his hair fell in his face. Okay, so I *was* thinking about those things, at least a little bit. And that made me even madder. Jerkboys aren't supposed to be cute, and you're not supposed to think about how nice and soft their lips look. But this one was, and I was.

Still, he *had* ruined my life, so he was definitely off-limits as far as the whole "I wonder what it would be like to kiss him" thing went. Not that I'd ever really, actually, you know . . . kissed anyone. Besides my parents and some relatives, of course. Everyone's done that. I mean *real* people. Boys. I hadn't kissed a boy. But I'd thought about doing it. And now I was thinking about doing it with Jerkboy. Too bad I'd been such a spaz both times he saw me. No wonder he didn't like me. Ugh!

This is the thing about boys—they can be

really, really irritating, but you still think about what it would be like to kiss them. It's one of the great Mysteries of the Universe, as Shan calls anything you can't explain. Not that boys are all that mysterious. I mean, there's not a lot to figure out about a group of people who spend most of their time playing video games and acting like five-year-olds. What's mysterious is why any of us like them at all.

Since my thinking about kissing Jerkboy definitely did not make any sense, I decided to stop thinking about him. But that didn't work out so well. So then I tried picturing Megan's face every time I thought about him. I imagined her telling me what a loser I was, and I imagined Jerkboy standing behind her, laughing at me. That worked better, but it also made me even angrier. Now I was mad at Jerkboy *and* Megan.

I took it out on my peas during dinner. I don't much like peas anyway, so it was easy to imagine that they were Megan and Jerkboy as I stabbed them with my fork. It was actually really stress relieving.

"I hear you had a great first day on the job," my father said as I swallowed the Jerkboy and Megan peas and wiped my mouth.

"Yeah," I said, nodding my head. "It was a lot of fun."

My father totally missed the snarkiness in my tone. That's one of the cool things about him—he always assumes things are going great. Considering that he's an insurance claims investigator, you'd think it would be exactly the opposite. I mean, he spends all day looking at pictures of houses that have burned down and cars that have been in accidents, and reading stolen property reports. You'd think he'd be totally cynical. But he's not. In fact, he's probably the most optimistic person I know.

"She's fantastic with the dogs," my mother told my father. "I heard nothing but great things about her today."

I didn't point out that she'd heard only great things because she wasn't there when Megan showed up to get Tallulah. There was no point in ruining her good impression of my dog-watching skills. Okay, so maybe it wasn't entirely honest of me not to tell her about what happened, but bringing it up was just going to make her worry, and, really, would that do anyone any good? I didn't think so.

I did, however, change the subject. I got my father talking about stars. As in astronomy. My father is really into stars and planets and stuff, and from the time I was little, he's taught me about the constellations. It's bordering on science geekdom, I know, but I don't care. I think stars are cool. And getting my dad to talk about them meant we wouldn't talk about my day.

"I'm glad you reminded me," he said. "If it's clear tonight, we should be able to see Vulpecula, the Little Fox. Did you know Vulpecula contains the Dumbell Nebula, which is the easiest planetary nebula to see with a telescope?"

The Dumbell Nebula, I thought. *That's where I should live.* I let him talk for a few more minutes, then excused myself. I disappeared to my room to worry some more. Besides being angry at Megan and Jerkboy, I was also afraid that Megan might make good on her promise and tell everyone how I'd let Tallulah escape. I knew for sure she would tell her parents, and since they were friends with *my* parents, I figured I could pretty much count on my mother and father finding out eventually.

But it was other people I was more concerned about. What if Megan really *did* manage to convince other customers not to leave their dogs at Perfect Paws? The entire day care business would be over. And I knew she was totally capable of ruining someone's reputation. Once, when we were in sixth grade, Rachel Mankowitz said Megan's skirt was ugly. Megan got back at her by spreading a rumor all over school that Rachel padded her bra with Kleenex, and for the next two years everyone called Rachel "The Stuffer."

Thinking about it made me mad all over again. Why did Megan have to be so mean? She had everything she could possibly want. Her father ran the biggest law firm in town. They had a nice house. Megan always had new clothes. She was popular. Basically, she got whatever she wanted. But she was still nasty.

I've seen enough movies to know that girls

like Megan are supposed to end up being misunderstood people who just want a real friend. Well, Megan isn't like that. She's nasty all the way through, like a solid milk chocolate Easter bunny made out of meanness.

I tried to distract myself from my depression by reading after dinner. I was working my way through a Jane Austen book, *Pride & Prejudice*, which I'd decided to read after seeing the completely amazing movie with Keira Knightley. She plays Elizabeth Bennet, who falls in love with this dreamy guy named Mr. Darcy. At first, the two of them make each other crazy because they're always arguing. But then they realize they're in love, and that's when things get really interesting. If you haven't seen or read it, you're only missing one of the best love stories ever.

Anyway, I read for a while, and I really did start to forget about how much Jerkboy and Megan were bugging me. A good book can do that. By the time I went to bed I was feeling almost okay about everything.

When I woke up the next morning the first

thing I saw was Rufus's big head. He was sitting beside my bed, waiting for me to get up. As I rubbed his ears, my first thought was that I was going to spend the day with dogs. The second thing I thought about was what had happened with Tallulah.

It was like someone poured a bucket of cold water over my head. I sat up and looked at Rufus. His tail was sweeping back and forth across the floor and his ears were perked up hopefully. "All right," I said. "I'm getting up."

Rufus jumped up and ran downstairs to get his breakfast as I stretched and tried to get excited about my day. Half an hour later, I walked with him over to Perfect Paws. My mother was already there, getting things ready for the first customers.

"It looks like you've got five dogs today," she said as I let Rufus into the backyard. "Three repeats and two new ones."

"Anyone I know?" I asked her.

"Pythagoras, Emmy, and Skunk will be here at nine," my mother told me. "The two new ones are coming in a few minutes. I don't know who they are. A man just called and said he'd heard good things about us."

She hadn't mentioned Tallulah, which was a relief. It meant that Megan hadn't called to complain. Yet. It was still early. But the news about the new customers made me feel better.

The two new dogs came in a few minutes later. They were both Chihuahuas, one brown and one black. The man with them was someone I'd never seen before.

"Good morning," I said. "Welcome to Perfect Paws." I knelt down to say hello to the dogs, who looked at me suspiciously and stayed near the man.

"Don't mind them," the man said. "They're always like this until they get to know you."

I held out my hand, and the brown Chihuahua sniffed it.

"That's Frida," the man told me. "Her companion is Diego. And I am Salvador Sanchez, the person fortunate enough to be their guardian."

"Well, Frida, you're very pretty," I said.

Frida's ears went up, and she wagged her tail at me.

"Ah, you know how to get her to like you," Mr. Sanchez said. "She's very vain. They both are."

"We're happy to have them here," I said, standing up. "Do they get along with other dogs?"

"Between you and me, they're very opinionated," Mr. Sanchez answered, speaking softly, as if the dogs might hear him and be offended. "They think Chihuahuas are the greatest of all dogs. But I've told them they must be on their best behavior for you."

"I'm sure everyone will love them," I said as I took the dogs' leashes from him. "When will you be back for them?"

"This afternoon around four o'clock," Mr. Sanchez informed me. "I teach history at the university, and today, unfortunately, I have a very long department meeting. I would take the little ones with me, but I fear their patience for such things is nonexistent. If the conversation is not about them, they are completely uninterested."

50

I laughed. "I'll try to make them feel important," I assured him.

"I'm sure you will," he said. "My friend Albert Wexman recommends you very highly."

So that was how he had heard about us. I was happy that at least one person thought I was good at my job. I made a mental note to thank Mr. Wexman when he brought Pythagoras in.

Mr. Sanchez left, and I let Diego and Frida loose in the back with Rufus. When he ran up to them, they stood side by side, their ears pointed up, and sniffed him cautiously. Then they turned around and ran off together. Rufus watched them for a minute, then threw himself down in the grass and started chewing on a tennis ball.

The other three dogs arrived one after the other, and by nine o'clock, everyone was in the back. I was happy when Frida and Diego ran up to Pythagoras and wagged their tails, as if they were happy to see him again. They ignored Skunk and Emmy at first, but pretty soon, everyone was playing with one another.

As the day went on, I relaxed more and more. Every time the phone rang I was afraid it was Megan or her parents calling to tell my mother about the Regrettable Incident. But when they hadn't called by noon, I decided the whole thing was behind me. Best of all, I knew I would never have to see Tallulah again, and that was fine with me.

As the dogs were picked up and went home, I congratulated myself on a successful second day. Everyone was coming back the next day, and we'd gotten two more calls from new customers.

That night at dinner, I didn't pretend my carrots were anything but carrots. I talked excitedly about my day when my father asked about it, and when my mother remarked how happy she was that the day care idea was taking off, I felt myself grinning. Maybe, I thought, it really would turn out to be a great summer after all.

Then my father dropped the bomb.

"I almost forgot," he said as I was reaching

for my second piece of fried chicken. "I signed us up for the Family Frolic at the club this weekend."

"You did?" I asked, hoping he was kidding.

"What?" he said. "You love Family Frolic."

Let me stop right here and say that I do *not* love Family Frolic. Okay, maybe I liked it when I was six, but that was before I realized how totally humiliating it could be.

Family Frolic is this thing they do at the country club my parents belong to. When I say country club, I don't want you to get the wrong idea. This isn't some totally fancy place that only rich people belong to. The Oak Club is nice and all, but it's not like everyone wears big white hats and drinks tea or anything. It's more like a social club. There's a pool, a golf course, and tennis courts, and there's even a pond you can row boats on. Most people in town belong to it.

The club holds Family Frolic once a year. What happens is, families compete against one another in different games, like horseshoes, badminton, three-legged races—that kind of thing.

The big event is a softball game in the after-noon. It's supposed to be a chance for everyone to get to know their neighbors and for families to bond, but really it's just totally hideous in the most embarrassing, cringeworthy way, especially if you're a kid.

"Do we have to go?" I asked.

"Yes, we have to go," my father said. "It's fun."

Fun for you, I wanted to say. But he seemed so into it that I kept quiet, gnawing at my chicken leg instead. I actually like going to the club, but only with Shan to use the pool. Otherwise, I'm not so into it. And one big rea-son I'm not into it is because Megan is there almost all the time. She and her friends like to hang out by the pool drinking Cokes, reading gossip magazines, and trying to get the college guys who work as lifeguards during the sum-mer to pay attention to them. I don't think I've ever seen any of them actually swim.

But my father was apparently all excited about it. And anyway, he's spent enough time taking me to movies he probably would never have gone to see if it had been up to him, and driving me to soccer practice and games and stuff. The least I could do was go to Family Frolic.

Besides, I told myself, *how bad could it really be?*

Chapter Five

O n Wednesday I got to Perfect Paws a little bit early so that I could help my mom set up for the grooming appointments, since we had more than the usual number signed up. I put out stacks of towels and made sure the shampoo and conditioner bottles were filled. I only had three dogs registered for day care, so I was looking forward to maybe helping out with some of the grooming, too. Playing with the dogs was fun, but actually doing hands-on stuff would be even better.

"Mrs. Trumble is bringing Charles in first thing," my mother told me as she laid out her clippers and combs.

I rolled my eyes. Mrs. Trumble and Charles are probably our least-favorite customers. Well, Mrs. Trumble is, anyway. Charles is actually a sweet dog. He's a Pekingese, so his fur needs to be trimmed regularly or it grows in his eyes. He's good about letting you cut it, but Mrs. Trumble always hovers around, telling you you're cutting it too short and letting out these little gasps whenever you put the scissors near Charles's face, like you're going to poke his eye out or something. It's incredibly annoying, and no matter how nicely you suggest that maybe she should go out for a while and come back in an hour, she never gets the hint.

At a quarter to nine, Mrs. Skelton came in with Skunk. I smelled him before he even got to the door, and I could tell by the look on Mrs. Skelton's face that Skunk had run into one of his little friends.

"I'm so sorry," Mrs. Skelton said as Skunk

sat beside her, looking guilty. "It happened on his walk this morning, and I don't have time to bathe him before I go to work. Do you mind?"

"Of course not," I told her. "I'll put him in the tub and have him smelling good as new in no time."

"Thank you so much," said Mrs. Skelton, sighing. She looked down at Skunk, who shook his head and yawned, like he didn't know what all the fuss was about.

"Come on, Skunk," I said, taking his leash and leading him toward the tubs. He's been through the drill so many times that he hopped up onto the wooden platform beside the tub and climbed right in.

As I was rubbing the shampoo into Skunk's fur, Pythagoras came in with Mr. Wexman, followed by Mr. Berd and Figaro. All four of them sniffed the air, then looked at Skunk, who was now covered in soapsuds.

"Hey," I said as I started to rinse the shampoo away. "You can let the boys out back. I'll be done in a minute."

As I was putting the special antistink rinse

on Skunk, I heard the door open. Assuming it was Mrs. Trumble and Charles, I didn't look up, hoping my mother would help her.

"Ah-hem," said a voice, sounding annoyed.

I turned around. Standing behind the counter was Megan. She was holding Tallulah in her arms.

"Oh," I said. "It's you."

"Yes, it's me," Megan said sarcastically.

I looked around for my mother, who was busy in the back of the shop and hadn't noticed Megan yet. I knew Megan was there to tell her what had happened, and I felt sick to my stomach. Behind me, Skunk was whining. He hated the smell of the rinse, and I wanted to get it off him. But first I had to get rid of Megan.

"Listen," I said. "About—"

"I want to leave Tallulah here for the day," Megan interrupted.

I hesitated. "You do?" I said. "Here?"

Megan sighed like I was wasting her time. "I don't *want* to," she said. "But you're the only place around."

"What about Dapper Dog?" I suggested,

naming the grooming salon a couple of towns over.

"I thought I'd be nice and give you a second chance," said Megan. "Anyway, you owe me. So here."

She thrust Tallulah at me. I had to take her. She looked at me and growled.

"I'm going to the club for the day," said Megan. "I'll get her around four. Try not to lose her this time."

Before I could say anything, Megan left. As the door shut behind her, my mother walked up. She looked at Tallulah. "Another repeat customer," she said as Tallulah dug her nails into my arm. "Great."

"Yeah," I said. "Really great."

I put Tallulah outside, where she immediately ran to the place where she'd dug under the fence. I'd filled it in, but you could still see that someone had been digging there. Tallulah scratched at it for a moment, then trotted off to take a toy away from Pythagoras. I figured that would keep her busy for a while, so I went back to finish bathing Skunk.

As I dried Skunk, I asked myself why Megan would leave Tallulah with me after what happened. I didn't for a second believe her claim that she was giving me a second chance. Megan Fitzmartin didn't give people second chances. She didn't even give them *first* chances. There had to be another reason. Very possibly, her business wasn't wanted at Dapper Dog.

I didn't have long to think about it. Once Mrs. Trumble arrived with Charles, the day got crazy. It was one dog after another. As I helped my mother wash, dry, comb, and trim the parade of dogs, I went out back every few minutes to make sure everybody—especially Tallulah—was okay. A couple of times I caught her nipping at the big dogs, but as long as she didn't try to escape again, I figured that was good behavior for her.

At lunchtime I took a break to eat the peanut butter and jelly sandwich I'd made before coming to the shop. I was halfway through it when someone came through the front door. I stood up, trying to swallow the bite of sandwich in my mouth, and immediately started choking. I coughed loudly.

"Are you okay?"

I finally got the sandwich down, then looked up at the worried customer. "I'm okay," I said. "Thanks for asking."

"No problem," Jerkboy said.

I couldn't believe he had just shown up in my life. Again. It was like it was fate or something. And he looked so good. The dirty overalls were gone and he was wearing jeans and an untucked white shirt with the sleeves rolled up almost to his elbows. His tan looked great against the white material, and for a moment I forgot that he was a jerkboy. Then I came to my senses.

"What are you doing here?" I exclaimed, and not very nicely.

"Barkley needs a bath and a trim," he said.

I looked over the edge of the counter. Sitting at Jerkboy's feet was a handsome springer spaniel. His black-and-white coat was dirty, and there were some tangles in his fur.

"He likes to roll in mud," Jerkboy told me, smiling.

"I can tell," I said, trying to sound cold

shoulderish. "Okay, we can do that."

"Great," said Jerkboy. "What time should I come back?"

Never, I wanted to say. But I told him, "He'll be ready at two."

"I'll be back at two then," he said. "Barkley, you be a good boy."

Barkley gave a little woof and Jerkboy patted him on the head. He handed me the leash, and I avoided looking at his eyes as I led Barkley to the back. For a second I thought Jerkboy was going to keep standing there, like he was waiting to say something. But when I looked back again, he was heading out the door.

I put Barkley into one of the washing tubs and turned the water on. While I waited for it to warm up, I took Barkley's collar off so that it wouldn't get wet. As I laid it down, I looked at the tag hanging from one of the metal loops. It was shaped like a bone, and Barkley's name was engraved on it. Beneath his name was another name and an address.

"Jack McKenna," I read. So Jerkboy had

a name. Jack. "That's pretty close to 'jerk,'" I said to Barkley.

Barkley behaved perfectly as I washed him. He didn't even mind when I washed his head. Most dogs hate that. But he stood there as I covered his eyes with my hand and sprayed the water on his face. As I rinsed the rest of him, I said, "How can such a jerk have such a nice dog?"

Barkley didn't answer me, but he turned and looked at me with his big, sad eyes. "Don't do that," I told him. "Your friend Jack has eyes like that."

I dried Barkley, then I asked my mother if I could practice my trimming skills on him. She agreed, and stood watching while I worked. First I used the clippers to trim the hair on his neck, head, and muzzle. Then I switched to the scissors and worked on his ears before moving on to his feet. Feet are the hardest, especially on dogs with fluffy legs. Barkley had a lot of fur there, and it took me a long time to get it right. But finally I was done.

"He looks good," my mother said. "You might want to take some more off his hocks and trim the feathers on his legs a little more, but not too much. That hair takes longer to grow back than the rest of his coat, so you don't want to overdo it."

I did what she suggested, and when I was finished, Barkley looked great, if I do say so myself. I was snipping the last stray hairs from his ears when Jerk—I mean Jack—came back.

"Wow," he said as he inspected Barkley. "You did this yourself?"

I nodded. "I'm not that good," I said. "I've only been doing it for about a year. My mom is the real pro."

"He looks fantastic," Jack said. "Really fantastic."

"Oh, well, thanks," I replied as I lifted Barkley down from the grooming table. "He held still. It helped a lot."

Jack knelt and ran his hands over Barkley. The dog shook himself, sending some little pieces of hair flying. Jack laughed and rubbed Barkley's head. "You look great, buddy," he said.

Watching them together, I couldn't help but smile. Jack clearly loved Barkley a lot, and Barkley loved him. Then I remembered that he'd snitched on me to Megan, and I got all businesslike. "That'll be twenty dollars," I said.

Jack reached in his pocket and handed me a twenty and a five. "The five's for you," he said. "You know, a tip."

"Thanks," I said, not really knowing what to do with the money. Finally I shoved it into my back pocket.

Then Jack said, "I guess we should go. I need to hit the library before it closes. You don't happen to know where it is, do you?"

"Three blocks down," I told him. "On Parson Street."

"That would be left or right when I walk out of here?" asked Jack.

"Left," I said.

"Sorry for the stupid question," said Jack.

"I just moved here. I don't really know where anything is."

"Where'd you move here from?" I asked him, surprised at myself. A second before, I'd wanted him out of the shop and out of my sight. Now I was asking him questions about himself.

"Chicago," he said. "Well, not really Chicago, but near it. It's just easier to say Chicago."

"Right," I said.

"I thought you said left," he said, smiling.

I laughed. He wasn't just cute, he was funny, too. Then I reminded myself that I was mad at him, and I made myself stop. *He is* not *charming,* I told myself sternly.

"I don't suppose you know anything about the Oak Club, do you?" Jack asked me.

"Sure," I said. "My parents belong to it. Practically the whole town does. Why?"

"My parents joined," Jack explained. "They want me to go to this thing there this weekend so I can meet people. The Family Circus or something, I think it's called."

"The Family Frolic," I corrected him.

"That's it," said Jack. "Is it as bad as it sounds?"

"Worse."

"Great," said Jack. He paused a second. "Are you going?" he asked me.

"I don't know," I lied. What was with all the lying these days? "Maybe. Probably."

"Then maybe it won't be all bad," said Jack.

Barkley whined. Jack looked at him. "I think someone needs a walk," he said. "I'll see you later."

"Bye," I said. "Bye, Barkley."

The two of them left. When they were gone, I leaned against the grooming table. I couldn't figure Jack out. On one hand, he was a total jerk for turning me in. And he'd been so condescending—like he knew more about dogs than I did! On the other hand, he was really sweet to his dog, and he'd been pretty nice to me too. It was like there were two different Jacks running around, one good and one bad. And both of them were really cute.

"Who was that boy?" my mother asked, coming in with a pile of towels.

"Oh, just some guy," I answered. "He's new here."

"He was very good-looking," said my mother, folding a towel.

"You think?" I said. "I didn't really notice."

My mother looked at me and raised one eyebrow, but she didn't say anything. I could feel my face turning red. "I think I hear Tallulah barking," I said, needing an escape from the situation. "I should go check on her."

Tallulah, much to my amazement, was fine, and so were the other dogs. I sat down on the back steps and watched them run around. Pythagoras trotted over and sat beside me, leaning his big body against me. I put my arm around him.

"You dogs have it pretty easy," I said. "You just sniff each other and figure out who you like and who you don't. It's a lot harder for people."

Py put his head on my knee, leaving a long string of drool on the leg of my jeans. I sighed and patted his big back. I was so confused. Jack made me feel all weird and nervous whenever he was around. It was clear I couldn't trust him. So why did I still think about him? And why did it make me happy that he'd said my being at the Family Frolic would make it less horrible?

"I'm acting like such a stupid girl," I told Py. "It's really not acceptable. What am I going to do?"

Py let out a big sigh and drooled some more.

"Thanks," I said. "You're a lot of help."

Chapter Six

The next day I was so busy at work that I barely had time to think about anything but dogs, dogs, and more dogs. In addition to the six dogs who came to day care, we had nine grooming appointments. From the minute I got there to the minute we closed at six I was washing dogs, brushing dogs, walking dogs, petting dogs, and sweeping up hair from dogs. I'd been afraid that Megan would show up with Tallulah again, but, thankfully, she didn't.

Even though I was so incredibly busy, I still managed to drive myself crazy by thinking about Jack. I tried not to, but every so often he'd just pop into my head. I couldn't help myself. I kept replaying what he'd said the day before about my being at the Family Frolic: "Then maybe it won't be all bad."

What had he meant by that? I wondered. Did he mean it would be nice to have someone he sort of knew there? Or did he think I'd do something embarrassing again? Was I simply amusing to him? Or did he mean hanging out with me was at least better than having to play a bunch of stupid games? Or did he mean something more? As in Something More.

I stopped myself right there. Something More was too crazy to even think about. Still, I thought, he *might* have been hinting around at something else. But what might that be?

There I was, giving Wendell and Walter their baths. They were both covered in soap, and they weren't happy about it. They were taking turns trying to jump out of the tub, and grabbing them was like trying to hold on to greased piglets. But I wasn't worried about them; I was worried about Something More.

I've already revealed my tragic never-been-kissed status. But it was worse than that. I was also a member of the never-had-a-boyfriend club. The two things kind of go together, so that probably doesn't come as a total shock. Sure, I'd had sort-of boyfriends when I was, like, seven. But basically that meant the guy would pull my hair during recess or call me "booger head." They didn't count. And I'd gotten Valentines from all the boys in my class, but so had everyone else. It wasn't like a guy had ever given me one that was *only* for me.

I knew that kissing was in my future, though, even if I didn't know who else it would involve. And something that important needs to be perfect. You can't go around kissing any guy who comes along, just to get it over with. You have to wait for the right guy. Because what if it's all bad and you don't like it? Then you're not sure if it's the guy, or you, or kissing in general. Who needs that kind of pressure?

I bet guys don't worry about this stuff. I bet they just find a girl, kiss her, and then think they're all studly because somebody let them put their lips on hers. *They* probably don't worry about bumping noses with a girl when they kiss her, or wonder how you know when to breathe. Guys are probably born knowing this stuff. Or maybe there's some secret meeting where someone explains it to them. Maybe on that awful day when the gym teachers split you up and the girls get The Talk about periods and blossoming into young women, the boys are getting the lowdown on kissing. It's so not fair. Not only do boys not have to get periods or wear bras, they don't seem to have to worry about the whole kissing thing, either.

Thinking about all the potential for major embarrassment, I decided I hoped Jack hadn't meant Something More. I wasn't sure I was ready. I needed some more practice time, like an athlete getting ready for the Olympics. Not that it is all that easy to practice kissing without a boy to do it with.

I finished washing Walter and Wendell, and when Mrs. Dibberson came in to get them she couldn't stop gushing about how great they looked. That was nice to hear. And she wasn't the only one who was happy. Pretty much every single person who had a dog at Perfect Paws that day said how impressed they were with how their dogs turned out. By the time the last one left I was feeling really good about myself, and the whole thing with Jack didn't seem like that big of a deal.

That night, after dinner, I was in my room reading when the phone rang.

"Allie, it's for you," my father called up the stairs.

I went down and took the phone from him.

"Hey, girlfriend," said a familiar voice.

"Shan!" I said. Actually, I sort of yelled it, because I was so excited to finally hear from her.

"How are you doing?" Shan asked me.

"I'm doing good," I told her.

"You mean you're doing *well*," Shan said in her best schoolteacher voice. Shan is big into grammar, probably because her father is an English teacher, and although it annoys me when she corrects mine, I let it go.

"Why haven't you called?" I demanded.

Shan sighed. "I haven't had two seconds to myself since I got here," she said. "My grandparents have me running around all the time. We've ridden the cable cars, taken the tour of Alcatraz, and driven down the crookedest street in the world at least three times. Last Sunday we went to Chinatown for dim sum, and it took four hours because it turned out my grandfather and the owner of the restaurant knew each other in Hong Kong. You won't believe this, but he kept asking me questions in Cantonese, and when I couldn't answer him, my grandparents decided I needed to take Chinese lessons! So now I have to do that two hours a day."

I laughed. "Have you learned anything?"

"*Ngoh m-ming,*" said Shan.

"What does it mean?" I asked her.

"It's either 'I don't understand' or 'I'm allergic to your pig,'" she said. "I get them mixed up. Anyway, what's going on there?"

"Well," I said hesitantly. "There's kind of this guy."

"A guy?" Shan said, sounding totally

excited. "Who? When? How?"

"His name is Jack," I told her. "He's new here. He's, I don't know, kind of cute, I guess."

"You guess?" said Shan. "That's not exactly a two-thumbs-up endorsement."

"Okay, so he's *really* cute," I admitted. "But I don't know. There's sort of this problem."

"What kind of problem?"

I explained the whole Tallulah incident to Shan. When I was done, she said, "That was a real jerkboy thing to do."

"I know," I agreed. "But then other times he's so nice. I don't know what to think. He's going to be at the Family Frolic this weekend, so maybe I'll get to spend some more time with him and see."

"Well, I have news in the boy department, too," Shan said.

"Spill it," I ordered her.

"Well," she said in a low voice, "there's this guy who lives a few houses down from my grandparents. His name is Hector. He's really funny."

"Why are you whispering?" I asked.

"I don't want my grandmother to hear me," she said. "If she knew I was talking to boys, she'd have a fit. She acts like I'm still ten years old. Whenever Hector sees us, he always says, 'Hello, Mrs. Chan,' really politely, and she just looks at him like he might try to snatch her purse or something."

"How do you talk to him, then?" I asked her.

"On my way home from Chinese class," said Shan. "He sits on the steps outside his house. My grandmother always takes a nap in the afternoon, so I get to talk to Hector for a while before I have to go in."

"A forbidden love affair," I said. "That's totally romantic."

Shan giggled, which surprised me. Shan never giggles. She says it's way too girly. But she had, and I knew that meant she was really into Hector.

"Do you think you and Hector will, you know, kiss?" Like Shan, I whispered the last word. I don't know why. It just felt so funny to say it.

"No!" Shan said. "No way. I mean, well, I guess it could happen if he wanted to."

"That means *you* want to," I teased.

"I didn't say that!" Shan objected. "That's not fair."

"It's okay. I mean, I guess I wouldn't mind if Jack and I . . ." I stopped. I just couldn't say it out loud, even if I was thinking about it.

Shan sighed again. "Maybe we both will," she said. "Wouldn't that be cool?"

"Maybe," I said doubtfully. I was already nervous that I'd let someone else know about Jack, even though it was my best friend. It made it all more real somehow. Before, it had just been in my head.

I heard voices in the background on Shan's end of the phone.

"That's my grandmother," Shan said. "I've got to go. Apparently, I'm going to learn how to make dumplings. Lucky me."

"Give me your number," I said. "Then I can call you next time."

Shan read me the number, and I scribbled it on a piece of paper. I promised to call her in a few days, then I hung up. As soon as I did I felt lonely. It was great talking to her, but I still missed having her right there. Especially now that I was in the middle of a boy crisis.

I picked up Fuzzy Wuzzy. He's this stuffed bear I've had since I was really little. I used to take him everywhere with me, dragging him around by the paw until I was big enough to carry him. A lot of his fur is worn away now, but he's still in pretty good shape. I keep him on my bed, which I know some people would think is kind of babyish for someone my age, but seeing him there makes me feel good.

"What am I going to do about this?" I asked Fuzzy Wuzzy.

Of course, he didn't answer.

"What if he does want to kiss me?" I said.

I looked at Fuzzy Wuzzy's face. I pretended he was Jack. What if I was standing there looking into Jack's eyes? What would I do?

Suddenly, I kissed Fuzzy Wuzzy. I closed my eyes, and I put my lips on his. Well, he doesn't really have lips, but he has this sort-of mouth that's sewn in black thread. So I kissed that.

It felt weird. I put Fuzzy Wuzzy down.

"There's no way I can do that with a real boy," I said. "No way. I'd die."

That's when I decided that under no circumstances was I going to kiss Jack McKenna.

Chapter Seven

When I woke up on Saturday morning, I hoped it was raining. Pouring rain. With thunder and lightning. That way I wouldn't have to go to Family Frolic. But it was sunny. Not only that, there wasn't a cloud in the sky. It couldn't have been a more perfect day for being outdoors. Thinking dark thoughts about Mother Nature, I dragged myself out of bed.

By ten o'clock I was helping my parents unload the car at the Oak Club. My mother staked out a picnic table she liked, and I carried our basket over.

"Hey there. Mind if we share your table?"

Jack was standing beside me, holding a cooler. He was wearing khaki surfer shorts, a light blue T-shirt, and a Seattle Mariners baseball cap. As soon as I saw him I felt better. Actually, I felt kind of gurgly in my stomach, but not a bad kind of gurgly. He acted totally relaxed, which of course made me even more nervous.

"No," I said. "I mean, no, I don't mind if you share. The table. With us."

"Great," Jack said, putting the cooler down. "Mom. Dad. Over here," he called to two people walking toward us.

Mr. and Mrs. McKenna came over. I could totally tell they were Jack's parents because it was like he'd gotten half of his looks from each of them. His mother was tall, like Jack. She had the same friendly smile, and her nose turned up a little at the end, just like Jack's did. But Jack definitely got his hair and eyes from his dad, although Mr. McKenna's hair was a lot shorter and he was wearing glasses.

Jack said, "This is Allie. She's the one who gave Barkley the great cut."

"Oh," said Mrs. McKenna, smiling. "It's so nice to meet you. Barkley looks very handsome."

"We're going to share a table with Allie," Jack told his mother.

"I'm sorry, honey," Mrs. McKenna said. "I already told the Fitzmartins we'd sit with them. Megan invited us. Allie, I hope that's all right?"

"Sure," I said, feeling my stomach gurgle again. This time, it *was* in a bad way. Just hearing Megan's name made me sick.

Jack looked at me. "Sorry about that," he said as his parents walked over to the Fitzmartins, who had taken a table three over from ours. "I didn't know. Anyway, I'll see you on the field."

He left, and I got busy unpacking the picnic basket. It was really too early to be putting any food out, but I needed something to do. I could hear Megan's voice as she greeted Jack and his parents, and I didn't want to think about what she was saying to them.

"Hey," my father said, coming up and waving a piece of paper at me. "Guess what's up first?"

"I don't know," I said, completely not interested.

"The three-legged race," he informed me. "Think we can take first place?"

I wanted to tell him that a three-legged race was the last thing I wanted to do. Every year for three years we had entered and every year we'd lost, twice to Megan and her father. But, as usual, my father seemed to think that this year things would be different. I could practically see him putting the trophy on the mantle over the fireplace. He looked so excited about it that I knew I couldn't disappoint him. All I could do was nod and try to seem like I didn't want to drop dead on the spot.

Fifteen minutes later, he and I were standing at the starting line. My left leg was tied to his right one, and his arm was around my waist. Next to us, Megan and Mr. Fitzmartin were tied together by the opposite legs, so that Megan was right beside me.

"I bet we win again this year," Megan said loudly to her dad. I knew she'd said it for my benefit, and wasn't surprised when she looked over at me and gave me a smirk that was supposed to look friendly, but which I knew wasn't at all. "Good luck," she said.

Jack and his father came hopping up and took the position on our other side. Jack leaned forward and looked over at me. "Good luck," he said, and unlike Megan, he sounded like he meant it.

"You too," I told him.

When the whistle blew, my father and I hopped forward. It took a few steps before we got our rhythm going, but then we did pretty well. In fact, when I looked around, I saw that we were actually ahead of everyone else.

Suddenly, I wanted to win. Despite everything I felt about Family Frolic being uncool, at that moment it was vital to the well-being of the entire planet that my dad and I win. I saw Megan and her father a step behind us. Megan was huffing and puffing as she tried to catch up. More than anything in the world, I wanted to beat her. Also, I wanted Jack to see me win. He and his dad were having a hard time coordinating their jumps, and they were way behind us. I didn't want to beat Jack, but I wanted him to see me beat Megan. Right then I realized that I wasn't just competing with Megan for a stupid ribbon; I was competing with her for Jack's attention.

"Come on!" I said to my dad. "Let's win this!"

We hopped faster, moving our single tied-together leg forward as quickly as we could. The finish line was only about ten feet away, and I knew we would cross it first if we could just keep going. I focused on the line and tried to block out everything else.

I guess I blocked out too much, though, because all of a sudden we were falling. I don't know if one of us tripped on something or what. All I know is that one second we were about to win and the next second I was eating grass. I was facedown on the ground, and I couldn't even turn over because I was tied to my father.

Someone came over and cut the rope that

was holding us together. I rolled over just in time to see Megan and her dad cross the finish line. They raised their arms in victory.

"Well, we almost did it," my father said, putting his arm around me.

Almost. But almost wasn't good enough. Megan took her trophy and waved it around for everyone to see, while I got up and tried to brush the grass stains from my shorts. *Megan, one. Allie, zero,* I thought as I walked back to the picnic table.

Things only got worse. As the day went on, Megan made sure that any time an event was for teams of two, Jack was her partner. Badminton. Horseshoes. A lame treasure hunt where we had to find things hidden around the club. Every single time, Megan and Jack paired up.

And what made it all really, really terrible — at least for me — is that Jack didn't seem to mind. Whenever I looked over at him and Megan, he was laughing and having a great time. During lunch, I even saw him offer Megan a piece of fried chicken. From where I was sitting, it looked like he was practically *feeding* it to her.

I did win one thing—a watermelon-eating contest. I ate all three of my slices in just under three minutes, even with my hands tied behind my back. Not that I'm all that proud of that accomplishment. After all, showing a guy you can eat like a pig doesn't do much to increase his interest in you. Unless you really *are* a pig, I guess. Then it might be impressive. But somehow I didn't think seeing me with my face covered in watermelon juice would make Jack fall crazy in love with me. And when I saw Megan pointing at me and laughing, I knew it wouldn't. She hadn't entered the contest, probably because she was afraid to get dirty.

The final event of the day was the sunset softball game. Given the way the day had gone, it was no shock that Mr. Fitzmartin and my dad ended up being team captains. My dad picked me first, and Megan, of course, went to her dad's team. When it came time for Mr. Fitzmartin to make his second choice, I saw Megan whisper something in his ear. Then Mr. Fitzmartin called Jack to his team, and I knew

Megan had asked him to do it.

Once teams were chosen, we started to play. The game was okay, I guess. I usually love to play sports, but I was in such a bad mood, I didn't really pay a lot of attention. So when it came time for the last inning, I was totally taken by surprise when I realized the score was 11 to 12, in Megan's team's favor. Our team batted last, and I sat on the bench and watched as our first batter struck out. The second one hit a pitch into left field, and the runner got to second before the ball came back. Now if we could just get a good hit, we could score two runs and win.

One thing I forgot to mention—Megan was pitching. That wasn't much of a surprise. She'd played on our school's team for three years, and although it pains me mortally to admit it, she's pretty good. She knows it, too, and she was showing off. She kept pausing between pitches, concentrating like she was about to perform major surgery instead of throwing a stupid ball.

Our third batter hit a pop fly, which was caught for our second out. That meant we only had one more chance.

"Allie, you're up."

I looked at my dad. "What?"

"You're up," he said.

"But . . ." I said dumbly. What I didn't say was, "Are you crazy? There's no way we're going to win if you put me up there. I can't hit a home run." Like I said, I'm into sports, but I prefer soccer. Hitting things that are flying at my face isn't my forte.

"Go on," my father said before I could make him understand the gravity of the situation. "You can do it."

I picked up my bat and walked to home plate. Standing there, I looked out at Megan watching me. She had a satisfied grin on her face, as if she knew she'd struck me out before she'd even thrown the first pitch. Behind her, I saw Jack standing between first and second base.

I put the bat up and waited for Megan to throw the ball. When she did, I kept my eye on it, the way Ms. Quackenbush always told us to in gym class. Not that that had ever worked for me before, but I had to try. The ball was rushing at me. *Don't strike out,* I told myself, and swung.

I heard a loud "crack" as the bat hit the ball. Then I saw the ball flying away from me. Megan turned and watched it, a look of surprise on her face. I stood for a second, the bat still in my hand, watching her watch the ball. And at that very second, I realized how badly I wanted to show up Megan. Now I had my chance.

Someone shouted, "Run!," and I ran. I looked toward first base, which seemed really far away. Over in left field, the ball had soared over the player's head. It was good. I saw the runner on second head toward third.

I reached first base and turned. As I rushed toward second, I saw our runner round third. We were going to do it! We were going to win.

Then I saw Jack running toward me. His softball glove was held out, and inside it the ball was tucked like a big egg. *How did he get it?* I wondered as my legs pumped like crazy. But I still had a chance.

Everything seemed to move in slow motion as Jack ran at me. I saw second base. I heard people screaming for me to run faster. And then I felt Jack's glove brush my side. I turned and looked at him. He mouthed the word "sorry" as I stumbled to a stop in front of him. I was so flustered from having him touch me, I didn't realize what had happened.

"Out!" someone yelled. Then "out" again as Jack threw the ball to home plate before our runner got there.

It was over. We hadn't won. My chance to be the big hero had failed. Worst of all, Jack was responsible for our loss.

As Megan and her team congratulated one another, I walked to the bench, where my father stood smiling at me. "That was a great hit, sweetie!" he said.

"It's just a game," I told him as I walked away from the cheers of Megan and her teammates, most of whom were friends of hers from school. *Score another one for Megan,* I thought nastily.

Back at our picnic table, I was not happy to

find my mother talking to Mrs. Fitzmartin and Mrs. McKenna. When they saw me, my mother asked, "How was the game?"

Before I could answer, I heard Megan's voice say, "It was *great*. Really close. But the other team couldn't quite get it together to win."

"That's too bad," my mother said, as I ignored Megan and got myself a can of root beer from our cooler.

"We were just talking about the youth committee," Mrs. Fitzmartin said to Megan. "I think it would be nice if Allie joined."

Hearing my name, I turned around. "What's this youth committee?" I asked.

"Nothing," Megan said quickly. "You wouldn't be into it."

"The youth committee to help plan the club's Fourth of July celebration," Mrs. Fitzmartin said. "Megan is on it. She says it's a lot of fun."

"Actually, it's a *ton* of work," said Megan. She looked at me. "And we really have enough people," she added.

"Nonsense," said her mother. "They can always use more help."

"I think it sounds like fun, Allie," my mother said. "You should do it."

"Jack should, too," Megan's mom said to Jack's.

"Should what?" asked Jack, coming up and dropping his softball glove on the table.

"Join the club's youth committee," his mother answered. "They're planning a Fourth of July party."

"Oh, you should," Megan chirped.

"I thought you said there were already enough people," I said to her.

Megan ignored me. Jack looked at her. Then he turned to me. "I'll join if you join," he said.

Megan's smile faltered for a second. Then she said, "Great. We'll have so much fun."

"Allie?" my mother asked. "How about it?"

I looked over at Megan. She was glaring at me. I knew the last thing she wanted was for me to be on the committee. She especially didn't want me there if Jack was going to be around.

And I wasn't exactly feeling so great about Jack, either. He'd been pretty chummy with Megan all day, and because of him I'd lost the game for my team. But despite everything, the idea of getting to be around Jack, even if it meant having to put up with Megan, still appealed to me.

"Sure," I said, hoping I wasn't making the biggest mistake of my life. "I'd *love* to."

Chapter Eight

The rest of the weekend, I felt like I was on a roller coaster. One minute I was mad at Jack, and the next minute I couldn't stop thinking about how I'd felt when our hands touched. I was pretty much *always* mad at Megan, because as far as I was concerned she was to blame for everything bad in the world, including global warming and the destruction of the rain forests. But Jack I just couldn't figure out. Every time I thought maybe we were getting somewhere, he'd turn around and do something to make me think I was crazy for thinking that. I mean, if you like a girl, do you spend all day with her worst enemy? No. And you certainly don't tag her out when she's about to win the game, making her look completely stupid in front of everyone, including—again—her worst enemy.

I just wasn't sure Jack's cuteness factor was high enough to make me forget about his behavior. Rufus could get away with just about anything when he looked at me with his puppy dog eyes, but Rufus had never intentionally humiliated me in front of two dozen people. When he did things that made me mad it was because he was acting like a dog. But Jack wasn't a dog.

"Maybe that's the problem," I told Shan on Sunday night, when I finally got hold of her and had filled her in on the latest Regrettable Incidents. "Maybe Jack is just acting like a guy, and guys are just naturally defective."

"I don't know," said Shan. "Hector is really nice. He always makes me feel good when he talks to me."

"Thanks," I said. "I feel so much better now."

"Sorry," said Shan. "I wish I could tell you Hector was a jerkboy."

"You could at least lie," I told her. "Has your grandmother found out yet?"

"No," said Shan. "And I hope she doesn't. She's finding enough things to criticize about me."

"But you're perfect," I teased.

"Tell *her* that," Shan said. "So far, I don't know how to cook, I laugh too much, and my feet are *way* too big."

"Well, they are sort of huge," I said.

"She's only teasing," said Shan, ignoring me. "I know she doesn't mean anything by it. It's like a game Chinese grannies play. She had this friend over last night, and she brought her granddaughter with her. We had to sit in the living room and drink tea with them, and the whole time my grandmother and her friend talked to each other about how this other girl and I need to improve ourselves."

"Who won?" I asked.

"I think I did," said Shan. "I may have big feet, but apparently the other girl is lousy at playing the piano *and* she bites her nails."

"Ouch," I said. "Hey, I bet Hector doesn't mind your gigantic feet."

"We haven't discussed it," said Shan. "But he did ask me to go to a movie this week."

"How are you going to manage that?" I asked her.

"There's a Chinese film festival playing here," Shan said. "I might say I'm going to that."

"Lying and subterfuge!" I said. "I'm shocked and appalled."

"So am I," Shan said. "It's not like me."

"See what boys will do?" I told her. "We're better off without them."

"If they were all like your jerkboy, I'd have to agree with you," Shan said. "I hate to say it, but maybe you should just give up on him."

"I keep telling myself that too," I said.

We talked a little longer, then Shan had to go. Before I went to sleep, I thought about our different problems. She had a boy she liked, who liked her, but who she couldn't see without getting into trouble. I had a boy I saw a lot, and

I thought *maybe* I liked him and *maybe* he liked me, but I wasn't sure. I didn't know who had the bigger problem, me or Shan.

On Monday morning I arrived at Perfect Paws and looked at the sign-up sheet for the day care program. I saw a couple of familiar names, as well as a few new ones. That made me feel better. At least one thing in my life was going well.

I started organizing things for the day, putting out toys for the dogs and filling water bowls. As customers came in, I put the dogs in the back and watched to make sure they all got along. Rufus was there, along with Py and the Chihuahuas. The two new dogs, a corgi named Dash and an Irish setter called Maggie, had settled into the group right away, so I left everyone to play and went inside to see if my mother needed any help.

When I walked in, I saw her standing at the counter talking to Megan and Jack. Barkley and Tallulah were there, too.

"So, you'll be back around six then," my mother said as I stood behind them, not sure whether I should say something or just run back out into the yard.

Before I could decide, Jack turned around and his eyes looked right into mine. "Hey, Allie," he said, smiling a little.

"Hey," I replied. I couldn't help but notice how cute Jack looked. He was wearing shorts again, only this time he had on a Modest Mouse T-shirt. They're pretty much my favorite band ever, and finding out that Jack apparently liked them too made me like *him* even more.

Megan turned too, only she didn't say anything. Instead, she stepped closer to Jack. "We're going to Magic Mountain," she announced.

"Oh," I said. Megan was looking at me as if I should have more to say than that. But I didn't.

"You're going to love it," she said to Jack when I didn't respond to her. "We are going to have the *best* day. But you *have* to hold my hand on the roller coaster. I'm such a baby when it comes to those."

"Right," Jack said.

Megan looked at me and shook her head so that her hair fanned out over her shoulders. I thought about my hair. I hadn't even washed it that morning. I'd gotten up late, and had just managed to pull it back into a ponytail. I knew it didn't look so great, and Megan knew it too. Her hair-shaking was her way of letting me know she was prettier than I was, like a peacock spreading its tail.

"We should get going," Megan said. "We want to be there right when it opens. That way we have the whole day together."

Jack nodded good-bye, but didn't say anything. He and Megan left, and my mother handed Tallulah and Barkley to me. "What an attractive couple," she said.

"The people or their dogs?" I muttered.

I took Barkley and Tallulah into the yard and let them loose. Barkley, wagging his tail, went over to Dash. Tallulah took off after the Chihuahuas, who were playing with a red rubber ball. Tallulah snatched it and darted away, while Frida and Diego stood there, wondering what had happened.

Once again, I couldn't help thinking how much the dogs were like their owners. Like Megan, Tallulah was snippy and mean. Barkley, on the other hand, was playing gently with Dash, as if he was welcoming the new kid on the first day of school.

Was Jack really like him? I wondered. He sometimes seemed to be. But then I thought about him and Megan at Magic Mountain. I pictured them buying hot dogs and funnel cakes and going on rides together. I knew Megan had made up the story about being afraid of roller coasters. I'd gone to Magic Mountain with her once on a school trip, and she'd insisted on sitting in the very first car and holding her arms up on all the hills. She was just trying to get Jack to hold her hand.

That was the worst thing. Why couldn't Jack see what she was doing? Why was he falling for all of her tricks? Any girl could see right through Megan and her fakeness. Why couldn't a guy like Jack? He didn't seem stupid.

The only answer was that he didn't *want* to

see through her. Like so many other guys, he wanted to think she was the perfect girl. It didn't matter that she was mean and spiteful and a liar. She was pretty, and that, apparently, was enough to make her worth going out with.

The Chihuahuas had gone after their ball. They were standing near Tallulah, and Diego kept reaching his nose toward the ball. Every time he did, Tallulah snarled at him. Diego sat down and looked at Frida, as if he didn't know what else to do. I felt bad for them. All they wanted to do was play, and Tallulah was ruining their fun. She didn't even want the ball; she just didn't want them to have it.

While I watched, Barkley came over to the other three dogs. He walked right up to Tallulah, bent down, and started to take the ball in his mouth. Tallulah snapped at him. Instead of backing down, Barkley barked at her. Tallulah sat down, as if she couldn't believe anyone had woofed at her. Barkley picked the ball up, turned around, and dropped it in front of Frida and Diego. They looked at him, then at Tallulah. Then Frida took the ball, and the two of them ran off to play.

Barkley came over to me and sat down. I reached over and rubbed his big, soft ears. "That was a really nice thing you did," I told him.

He snuffled at my hand with his nose. Tallulah was looking at us with a nasty expression on her face, as if she wanted to bite us both.

"Why can't Jack be as smart as you?" I asked Barkley.

He looked up at me, woofed once, and wagged his stub of a tail. Then he ran off to see what Rufus and Py were doing, while I sat there and felt sorry for myself.

Chapter Nine

As I stood in front of the door to Megan's house and rang the buzzer, I felt like I was standing at the entrance to Dracula's castle. I would rather have been anywhere else than there, and I probably would have left, except my mother was with me and I couldn't exactly take off and leave her there by herself. Instead, I pasted a fake smile on my face, so that when Mrs. Fitzmartin opened the door, I would at least *look* like I wasn't in the middle of my worst nightmare.

"Hi," Mrs. Fitzmartin said as my mom and

I walked into the house. "Allie, Megan and the others are in the living room. You can just go on in."

"Thanks," I said, wishing I'd brought a garlic necklace and a long wooden stake with me, in case Megan turned out to be a vampire.

When I entered the living room, I saw Megan sitting on a big, white couch. She was surrounded by a bunch of girls I knew because we all went to the same school, but who I'd barely said six words to since first grade. They were Megan's best friends. Instead of using their real names, Shan and I called them the Megbots, since they all tried really hard to be exactly like Megan. They wore their hair like her. They dressed like her. And worst of all, they acted like her.

When they saw me, the Megbots looked at me for a second, then went right back to whatever it was they were talking about, as if I didn't exist. That was fine with me. I sat down in a chair as far away from them as I could get and waited for something to happen.

I didn't have to wait long. About five minutes after I got there, Jack showed up. As soon as he came into the room, Megan and the Megbots all started giggling like a bunch of crazy birds. Megan stood up and said, "Jack! I'm *so* glad you could come. These are my friends Sarahjessicashaunamelindaamberandbeth." She said their names like it was one long one, really fast, so that Jack couldn't really catch any of them. I wondered if she'd done it on purpose, so that she would be the only one who Jack really knew.

She didn't mention me at all, of course, and it took a while for Jack to turn and see me. When he did, his face lit up, like he was relieved to see someone he knew besides Megan. "Hey," he said, starting to come over to me. Before I could answer, Megan grabbed his hand and pulled him down onto the couch beside her.

"Am I the only guy on the committee?" Jack asked.

"No," one of the Megbots informed him. "But you're the only one coming tonight. The other three are busy with a baseball game or something."

"Oh," said Jack. "Well, lucky me."

The Megbots giggled some more. I rolled my eyes and sighed. I wished more than anything that I could just disappear. Since I couldn't do that, I wished that at least Shan was there with me to provide moral support. But Shan was on her date with Hector. Remembering that made me even more depressed.

"So then Jessica, not this one, the other one, showed up in *exactly* the same dress that Anna was wearing. It was so funny. And, of course, they both looked ridiculous in it. I mean, what were they thinking?"

One of the Megbots was talking. The others were all listening to her like she was telling them the meaning of life or something. Surrounded by them, Jack was nodding and sort of smiling, but it looked like he was starting to fall asleep. *They have him under their spell,* I thought to myself. *In a minute, he's going to nod off. Then they'll suck the blood out of him.*

"What *I* want to know," Megan said, her voice drowning out everyone else's, "is how

Jessica thought she could have a party and not invite *me*." She snorted, as if the idea was completely unbelievable.

"I *know*," said one of the Megbots. "Totally stupid, right?"

I couldn't take it anymore. "Hey," I said. "Aren't we supposed to be talking about the Fourth of July thing?"

They all turned and stared at me as if I'd grown another head. I stared back, and the Megbots all looked at Megan, like they didn't know what to do next.

"We were *getting* to that," said Megan. "But you're new at this, so I guess you don't know how things work."

The Megbots laughed. I saw Jack give me a little smile, as if he felt sorry for me. For some reason, that made me madder at Megan and her friends. I didn't want Jack to feel sorry for me. I wanted to be able to stand up to the Megbots and show them that I was better than them, and I wanted him to see it too.

"We really should discuss the Fourth of

July," Megan said, as if I hadn't said anything and she was the one getting everyone to focus. "We need a theme."

The Megbots all looked at one another, waiting for someone to say something. After a minute, one of them said, timidly, "Well, what's the point of the Fourth of July? That's when that boat dropped the first settlers off, right? On that rock?"

"The *Maypole*," another Megbot said.

The first Megbot nodded. "Yeah," she said. "Why don't we have everyone dress like pilgrims?"

"The Fourth of July has nothing to do with pilgrims, or the *May*flower," I said. "It commemorates America's independence from British rule."

The Megbots looked like I'd just said they were all wearing last year's clothes. But Jack nodded. "Allie's right," he said. "That's why they call it Independence Day."

"After the Will Smith movie," said a Megbot, her eyes going wide as she laughed at her own brilliance.

"I think it's the other way around," Jack told her.

"Anyway," said Megan. "Now that Allie's given us this *crucial* little history lesson, we still need to think of a theme. Remember, we're supposed to be raising money for a charity."

"I don't know why we can't just have a party," one of the Megbots complained. "Why do we have to *help* people. It takes all the fun out of everything."

"We just do," Megan said. "Last year they raised money for underprivileged kids. Or maybe it was for old people. Whatever."

The Megbots were silent. I guess they were trying to grasp the concept of actually helping other people. Maybe none of them had ever done anything for someone else.

"What about animals?" Jack suggested.

The Megbots all looked relieved that someone had said something. "Animals?" Megan asked.

"Yeah," said Jack. "We could raise money for the shelter. They always need help. We could, I don't know, have people bring their dogs to the party or something."

"I *love* it," Megan said. "Jack, that's the best idea ever."

"It's just a suggestion," said Jack. "You guys might have some better ideas."

"No," Megan said firmly. "The animals need our help, right, girls?"

The Megbots all nodded.

"I *love* animals," Megan said, then paused like she was waiting for someone to congratulate her. When no one did, she said, "Let's take a vote. All in favor of raising money for the shelter?"

The Megbots raised their hands, as did Megan and Jack.

"All right, then," said Megan. "That's it."

"What about Allie?" Jack said. "She didn't vote."

"Allie?" Megan said in a voice that was supposed to sound friendly. "What's your vote?"

"Sure," I said, surprised that they had even bothered to ask me at all.

"This is going to be so much fun," said Megan, going back to ignoring me. Then she gave a little shriek. Everyone looked at her. "Oh, you know what?" she said. "I just had the cutest idea. We can have people dress their dogs in costumes! That would be so great."

"Not for the dogs," I blurted out before I could stop myself.

"Did you say something?" Megan asked me.

"I said, it wouldn't be fun for the dogs. Dressing dogs up makes them feel ridiculous."

"Really?" Megan said. "And how do you know how dogs feel? Are *you* a dog?"

The Megbots giggled. Megan smirked at me.

"Maybe I know how they feel because I actually pay attention to them," I shot back. "I don't treat them like toys."

The smile melted from Megan's face. I could tell she wanted to say something really nasty. But Jack was sitting beside her, and I knew she wouldn't risk it while he was around.

"I think costumes would be adorable," said one of the Megbots. "I think dogs in coats and sweaters and things look sweet. Besides, they're *dogs*. They don't know any better."

I stood up. I was just about to tell the

Megbot that she was the one who didn't know any better. But before I could speak, Jack said, "I think costumes is too much. It's easier if people just bring their dogs without clothes. That way they can run around and play without getting all dirty."

"Jack's right," Megan said instantly. "We want the dogs to be able to play."

Jack's right? I thought angrily. When he said it, Megan acted like it was totally obvious that putting clothes on dogs was a bad idea. When I said it, I was being unreasonable. I looked at Jack. He was looking at me and nodding, as if to say, "We won!" But I wasn't about to let him think I was grateful, even if I was. He may have spoken up, but he was still sitting next to Megan. He'd taken *her* to Magic Mountain. And, most important, he'd still ratted me out to her. He could never be on my side if he was already on hers.

"Now that we have our theme," Megan said, "we can get back to talking about important stuff. Like what people are going to wear.

I think everyone should wear red, white, and blue."

"Whatshername from that show was wearing the cutest blue dress in *Teen People* this week," one of the Megbots said.

I tuned them out. Once Megbots started talking about clothes, I knew it was all over. You could set off dynamite next to them and they wouldn't even notice. It was just clothes, clothes, clothes, clothes, clothes. I knew there were other things we needed to talk about, like who was going to do what to actually make sure this event happened. But why should I care? I wasn't one of them. I didn't care about their club or their Fourth of July party. I was only there because my mother had made me come.

After another five minutes, I went to look for my mother. She was in the kitchen with Mrs. Fitzmartin.

"We're done," I told her.

"Already?" said my mother. "That was fast."

I hurried her out and into the car. As we

drove home, she asked me about the meeting. "Did you come up with a good idea?"

"We're raising money for the animal shelter," I answered.

"What a great idea!" said my mother. "I bet that was your idea."

I didn't say anything. The truth is, it *was* a great idea. It was a *fantastic* idea. And I was almost mad that I hadn't thought of it before Jack had. Why did Jack always have to act like he knew more about dogs than I did?

I looked out the window. I was the one who loved dogs. Not Megan. Not the Megbots. They couldn't care less about dogs. I knew that. But I still felt like I was the one who was the loser. And I knew that Jack was a big part of why I felt like that. I knew I shouldn't care whether he liked me or not. But I did. I wanted him to sit next to *me*. I wanted him to go with *me* to Magic Mountain.

I especially wanted the two of us to work on raising money for the shelter together. Our love of dogs was the one thing I knew we had in common. I pictured the two of us visiting the dogs whose lives we'd made better. Jack would look into my eyes and say, "We did it, Allie." He'd smile at me while the dogs barked, and then he would lean down and—

No. I wasn't going to think about *that*. I pushed the thought out of my mind.

At least the dogs would get something out of it, I reassured myself. That should have been enough.

But I knew it wasn't.

Chapter Ten

On Wednesday it was raining when I woke up. I'd left the window open a little when I went to bed, and when I stepped on the carpet, it was wet and cold. I slammed the window shut, trying to ignore the fat, gray clouds that covered the sky. As I turned my back on them, a grumble of thunder came from above, as if the sky was growling at me.

A hot shower and breakfast weren't enough to put me in a good mood, and even the thought of spending the day at Perfect Paws was unappealing. All I wanted to do was curl up in bed and hide. That's how bad the thing with Jack made me feel.

Because of the rain, I rode with my mother over to the shop. Part of me wanted to walk, to get soaking wet so that my outsides matched my insides. But I didn't need a cold on top of everything else.

"Are you okay?" my mother asked as we drove.

"Fine," I said.

"You don't look fine," she remarked.

"I'm just tired," I lied. "I didn't sleep very well."

"It's probably the storm," she suggested. "Your father kept waking up too."

Yeah, I wanted to say, *the storm inside my heart.* But I didn't want to talk about it with her. Or with anybody. There was no way to explain something that didn't really make sense. If I told her that, for some reason I couldn't explain, I really liked this guy who sometimes seemed to like me, but other times acted jerky—and liked someone else—she'd tell me to forget about him.

But I didn't want to forget about Jack. I just couldn't get him out of my head.

"Well, hopefully this will blow through soon and the sun will come back out," said my mother as she pulled up to the shop.

In spite of the rain, I had a lot of dogs come in that day for day care. There were five, not counting Rufus: Pythagoras, Skunk, and Emmy, who by now I considered regulars, and Maggie and Dash from the week before. Because it was raining, I decided to keep the dogs inside. Luckily, the area where we do all the grooming is really big. It has this waist-high retractable fence we can stretch across when we need to divide it into two spaces, and the dogs could hang out there. It was a little cramped, but it was better than having everyone out in the wet yard.

"Thank heavens there aren't any more," my mother said as she went over to the grooming table, where a nervous-looking little shih tzu was waiting to be clipped. "One more, and we'd be overrun."

As if that was the cue for her scene, Megan came in exactly as my mother finished talking. She was wearing a shiny pink raincoat, and Tallulah, who was in her arms, had on an identical one.

"I know you think dressing dogs up in clothes is cruel or something," Megan said as she put Tallulah on the counter. "But her fur gets all curly when it gets wet."

Like yours? I thought, eyeing her raincoat.

"I'll pick her up at four," said Megan. "I'm going to look at dresses for the Fourth of July party."

I didn't say anything. Not that Megan cared. She turned and walked out. I picked up Tallulah, who growled, and took the raincoat off her. When I set Tallulah on the floor, she took off after Dash, biting at his little stump of a tail.

"You don't like her, do you?" asked my mother, as I put the raincoat on a shelf.

"Tallulah?" I said. "She's okay. She's just high-strung. It's not her fault."

"Not her," said my mother. "Megan."

"Oh," I said. "No, not really."

"I don't blame you," my mother told me.

I turned around and looked at her, surprised. We'd never talked about Megan before, mainly because I didn't want my mother to think I didn't like her friend's daughter. "Really?" I asked.

My mother smiled. "She's not very nice," she said.

"No," I agreed. "She's not."

"Unfortunately," my mother said as she trimmed the shih tzu's bangs, "you have to deal with the Megans of the world. Especially if you have a shop like this one."

I sighed. "I know."

"It's not always easy," said my mother. "Believe me, there are times when I'd love to tell people what I think of them."

"Why don't you?" I asked her.

"Because it won't change them," she answered. "There's not much you can do when people act that way except try to ignore them."

"That's reassuring," I said sarcastically.

The rain stopped right after lunch, which

was a huge relief, as both the dogs and I were getting a little stir-crazy. There's only so much running around you can do inside a shop, and everyone was starting to get in everyone else's way.

I decided to take them all for a walk. The yard was still too wet and muddy for them to play in, but we could at least go to the park, which had paths to walk on. I leashed everybody up, then headed out the door, the seven dogs anxiously pulling at me.

Let me tell you, controlling seven dogs who have been cooped up inside all day isn't easy. But I managed to get everyone to the park. By then the sun was out, and people had come out along with it. The park was more crowded than I'd expected, with bikers and skateboarders crowding the walkways along with joggers and people just walking around enjoying the end of the storm.

I was starting to think that maybe I should turn around and head home, when a man came around a turn walking a French bulldog. When the bulldog saw all of my dogs, his ears stood up and he pulled at his leash, trying to get close enough to smell everyone.

"Sit," I said, and all my dogs sat down. All except Tallulah, who stood behind the big dogs, hiding from the bulldog.

"Are they all friendly?" the man asked me.

I nodded, and he let the little bulldog come up to Skunk, who wagged his tail.

"His name's Eiffel," the man said.

"Hi, Eiffel," I said. "Nice to meet you."

Eiffel was busy inspecting all the other dogs, and they sniffed him right back. Everyone was getting along well, when suddenly Tallulah lunged out from behind Rufus and bit Eiffel on the ear. Eiffel squealed and pulled away. Tallulah went after him.

"Tallulah!" I shouted. "No!"

She ignored me, trying to get at poor little Eiffel, who was running the other way. Tallulah pulled harder, and I felt her leash slip from my hand despite how hard I was holding it. As she tore away from me, Eiffel turned and snapped at her. She snapped back, and then they were both making a horrible noise.

This set all the other dogs off. All at once, they started barking crazily. Then they were pulling. I felt myself fall forward. As I panicked, I let go of the leashes. I watched as all the dogs ran off in different directions.

"Skunk!" I shouted. "Rufus! Maggie! Dash! Py! Emmy!"

They didn't listen. They were all worked up because of the fight between Tallulah and Eiffel. And I couldn't run after any of them until I broke that up.

"Get off!" Eiffel's dad was yelling. "Stop it!"

He had picked Eiffel up, but Tallulah was still jumping at him, snapping her teeth. Eiffel, terrified, huddled in the man's arms.

"Is he all right?" I asked.

"Just get this little monster away from us," the man said, kicking at Tallulah with his foot. She latched onto his shoe and shook her head.

I reached out and grabbed her. She turned and sank her teeth into my hand, but I ignored the pain. "I'm so sorry," I called to the man as I tried to see where the other dogs had gone.

He hurried off, carrying Eiffel. But my

problems had only begun. I could see the other dogs, but I wished I couldn't. They were all in some kind of trouble. Rufus and Skunk had run straight for the pond in the middle of the park. They were in the water, which was totally not allowed.

But at least they were out of the way. Emmy had managed to trip a jogger, who didn't see her and had gotten her foot caught in Emmy's leash. She was kneeling on the ground, looking at a scrape on her leg. Maggie had spotted a bird, and she was chasing it, barking her head off. Pythagoras was standing in front of a little girl who was holding an ice cream cone. Py's big tongue was lapping at the ice cream, while the girl cried. And Dash was running after a boy on a skateboard, his little butt bouncing up and down as he tried to keep up.

I didn't know where to start. I couldn't chase after all of them at once, and Tallulah was trying to squirm her way out of my arms. I wanted to cry, but I knew that wouldn't help.

"Is this your dog?" the mother of the little girl whose ice cream cone Py was eating called out.

"You need to get those dogs under control!" the jogger added.

"Don't you know the rules?" someone else shouted. "No dogs in the pond."

Everyone was yelling at me at once. Their voices surrounded me, and I couldn't tell who was saying what. All I heard was angry sounds ringing in my ears.

"Rufus!" I called out weakly. "Dash!"

"Looks like you need a little help," said a familiar voice.

I turned and saw Jack standing there with Barkley. Before I could say anything, he handed me Barkley's leash. "Here," he said. "You get the ones in the pond. I'll go after the runners."

Before I could answer, he was gone. I looked down at Barkley, who sat quietly, like he was waiting for me to do something. I watched Jack as he ran after Dash and Maggie. Where had he come from? I wondered.

I didn't have time to worry about it. I ran over to Py and grabbed his leash, pulling him away from the little girl, who looked down at her mostly eaten strawberry ice cream and the long slobbers of drool hanging from her hand and started crying again. Then I collected Emmy, who was trying to lick the jogger's skinned knee. Finally, I went to the edge of the pond and called for Rufus and Skunk to get out. After a few tries, they listened to me.

Once I had the dogs in hand, I went back to apologize to everyone. But they had all disappeared. I was sort of relieved about that, but I also felt terrible about what had happened. I wanted to let people know that it was all an accident, that these were *good* dogs. I especially wanted the little girl to know that. I didn't want her to be afraid of dogs because of this.

"Those dogs shouldn't have been in the pond," an old woman said, shaking her finger at me. "They chase the ducks."

"Yes," I said. "I know. I'm really sorry."

She shook her head and walked away. Then I saw Jack coming toward me. He had Dash and Maggie with him.

"Is this everybody?" he asked as he handed their leashes to me.

I counted. "Eight," I said. "Wait. That's not right."

"This one's with me," said Jack, taking Barkley's leash back. His fingers brushed mine, ever so briefly.

"Seven," I said. "That's right."

Suddenly, we were both quiet, like neither of us knew what to say next. Jack looked at me and started to speak, then looked away, as if he'd just seen something really interesting in the other direction. I knew I should thank him, but I couldn't find the words. It was a totally awkward moment, and I couldn't wait for it to be over.

Finally, he turned back to me. "You sure don't have much luck walking dogs," he remarked.

"What's that supposed to mean?" I snapped. It came out meaner than I wanted it to, but he'd taken me by surprise. I'd been expecting something, well, nicer, I guess. After all, I'd just been through a pretty big trauma. The least Jack could have done was make me feel better.

"You know, we met because—"

"I know how it happened," I said, interrupting him. "You don't have to remind me."

I was angry. I was also *really* embarrassed, which made me even more upset. Jack had helped me. Again. It was no wonder he thought I was a bad dog walker!

"I didn't—," he tried again.

"Thanks for your help," I said. "I'm sure you'll have fun telling Megan all about this."

I could feel my cheeks burning so I turned and walked away, pulling the dogs with me.

"Allie," Jack called after me.

I ignored him. "Come *on*," I said to the dogs, walking faster. "This is all of your faults in the first place."

They looked at me. I looked away. I knew I was taking out my frustration on them. As I walked back to Perfect Paws, I felt myself beginning to cry.

Chapter Eleven

" I hear you had an interesting time in the park yesterday."

I looked at Megan. She had just walked in, alone.

"Are you dropping Tallulah off?" I asked, ignoring her remark.

"No," Megan said. "I'm meeting Jack downtown to go shopping."

"So, you just stopped in to say hello?" I asked.

"I was walking by," said Megan. "It's no trouble."

"I'm sure it isn't," I said. I knew full well she had come by on purpose to make sure I knew that *she* knew about what had happened at the park.

"I'm so glad no one was hurt yesterday," Megan said. She didn't seem in any hurry to leave.

"Only the dog Tallulah bit," I told her.

Megan waved her hand at me. "She was just playing," she said. "She would never hurt anyone."

"Tell that to Eiffel," I snapped. "He's the one whose ear was bleeding."

"Eiffel?" Megan said. "What a dumb name."

"Megan, I'm kind of busy here," I said, trying to control myself. "Is there anything I can do for you?"

"Oh, no," she answered. "You've done so much already." She smiled her fake smile at me, and I smiled back, just as phonily.

"I'm curious," I said. "How did you hear about what happened in the park?"

"A friend," she said.

"A friend," I repeated. I knew that by *friend* what she really meant was Jack.

"I mean, *everyone* saw it," Megan continued. "It's not like there weren't people around. Anyway, I should be going."

You should have never come in in the first place, I thought.

"I'll tell Jack you said hi," she said as she walked toward the door.

"Why?" I said, surprising myself. Immediately, I wished I hadn't said anything. It was exactly what Megan wanted.

"What?" said Megan, acting shocked. "Don't you like Jack?"

"I don't know him well enough to say if I do or not," I said, wishing she would just get out and leave me alone.

"That's funny," said Megan silkily. "He says he runs into you all the time."

"Does he?" I asked.

Megan nodded. "While you're walking the dogs," she said. "Or maybe he said when you're *looking for* them."

I glared at her, and was just about to tell her

exactly what I thought about Jack McKenna, when my mother walked in from the other room, where she'd been washing some towels. "Hi, Megan," she said. "Did you bring little Tulip in for a trim?"

"No," Megan said sweetly. "*Tallulah* is at home. I just came by to say hello to Allie. I'm meeting a friend, though, so I should go."

"Okay," said my mom. "Say hi to your mother for me."

"I will," said Megan. "Bye, Allie."

"Bye," I muttered.

"I overheard your conversation," my mother said as soon as Megan was gone. "The last part, anyway. I thought I'd try to save you from any more of Megan's pleasantries."

My mouth fell open as I stared at my mom, and she grinned.

"Thanks," I said.

"Any time. So, what's this about the park, and what's going on with you and Jack?"

I groaned. Those were the last two topics I wanted to talk about. But I figured I owed my mom for helping get rid of Megan, so I told her the story about Tallulah, Eiffel, and the dogs getting loose. To my surprise, she started laughing.

"You're not mad?" I asked.

"Why would I be mad?" she said. "It was an accident. And it sounds like it was all little 'Tulip's' fault."

"It really was," I said, laughing at my mother's deliberate use of the wrong name for Megan's dog. "Still, I should have been more careful."

My mother reached out and pushed my hair back from my eyes. "Allie, you're the most responsible kid I know," she said. "Look at how well you've run this day care. Everyone tells me what a great job you're doing. Your father and I are really proud of you. Don't let one little thing get you down."

"I guess," I said.

"You guess?" said my mother. "Or you know?"

"I *know*," I said, trying to sound optimistic. But what I was thinking was, *Even* little *things can bite and sting.*

"Now, what about Jack?" my mom asked me.

"That's a whole other story," I replied. "I don't even know where to start."

"Do you like him?"

I shrugged. "That's the problem," I told her. "I sort of do. But then he does these things that are really jerkboy."

"Jerkboy?" my mother said.

"It's a Shanword," I explained.

My mother nodded. "What, exactly, has he done?"

"It's hard to explain," I said. "It's little things. But they add up to one big thing, which is that I shouldn't like him."

Thankfully, my mom didn't ask for details. Although I'd owned up to the incident in the park, I still hadn't told her about losing Tallulah the first time. I was pretty sure she'd be cool about it, but I didn't want to press my luck, especially when we were having a mother-daughter bonding moment.

"You think Jack is the one who told Megan

about the Regrettable Incident in the park," she said.

I laughed at her use of Shan's phrase. "I don't know who else could have," I said.

"Let me tell you something about boys," said my mother. "Sometimes you think they're one thing, when really they're something else."

I thought about it for a minute. "What?" I said. "That doesn't make any sense."

"I'm just saying, things aren't always what they seem," my mother said. "Like with the dogs yesterday. If someone didn't really know you, they might have seen that and thought you didn't know what you were doing."

"Thanks a lot," I said.

"Well, it's true," she said. "Right?"

"Yeah," I said reluctantly. "I suppose so. But I *do* know what I'm doing."

"That's my point," my mom said. "Anyone who really knows you would know that. But someone who just knew you a little tiny bit wouldn't."

"I'm still confused," I told her.

"Maybe how you feel about Jack is because of how you're looking at him," she said. "That's all."

I shook my head. "Sure," I said. "Okay. Whatever."

"Don't 'whatever' me."

I sighed. "*Okay.* I get it. I don't know who Jack really is."

"But you could fix that," my mother said.

"How?"

"Ask him out," she suggested.

"Mom!" I yelled.

"Why not?" she said, putting her hands on her hips and giving me one of her mom looks. "I asked your father out on our first date."

"You did?" I said, not sure I believed her.

"Yes," she answered. "He thought I didn't like him, so I asked him out."

"Why did he think you didn't like him?" I asked.

"Because a certain girl who also liked him told him I didn't," she said.

"But Jack spends all his time with Megan. They're practically *engaged.*"

"That's how it *looks*," said my mother.

"And it's what Megan says," I argued.

My mother gave me another look. "And do you trust Megan?"

"No," I said. "But I've seen how he is around her. He's like all the other Megbots."

"The what?"

"He acts like all her friends, like she's the best thing since text messaging."

My mother made a little snorting sound. "I still say you should ask him out," she said.

"No way," I told her. "*No. Way.*"

She looked over at me, but didn't say anything. I thought maybe I saw her smiling, but I wasn't sure. Anyway, I'd had enough of the conversation. I decided it was time to go check on the dogs.

They were fine. After the rainstorm, it had turned sunny and hot. Everyone was sleeping in the sun or in the shade beneath the tree. Rufus was sitting in the plastic wading pool I'd brought in and filled with water for the dogs to play in.

I sat on the steps and thought about what

my mom had said. Was I wrong about Jack? Was he really a great guy, and I just wasn't seeing the whole story? I didn't know. My mother had suggested asking him out, but that was easy for her to say! I just didn't know if I could do that.

Why not? said a voice in my head. It sounded an awful lot like Shan's. I pictured her standing in front of me, giving me the look she uses when she thinks I'm being completely ridiculous. *He's just a* boy, the voice said.

"You're right," I said out loud. Thinking I was talking to them, a couple of the dogs looked up at me for a moment before putting their heads down and going back to sleep. "He is just a boy," I said, more softly this time.

Chapter Twelve

"Things with Hector are going really well," Shan told me when I called her on Sunday night.

She'd said his name out loud, which surprised me. "Aren't you afraid your grandma will hear you?" I asked her.

"It's okay," Shan said. "She knows. I told her. At first she was upset, but then I had Hector come over for dinner. Now she's practically in love with him."

"Oh," I said. "That's amazing."

"Isn't it?" Shan said. She lowered her voice

143

a little. "We went to the movies last week, and he held my hand." Her voice was all breathy and weird. It didn't sound like Shan at all.

"He did?" I said. "Cool."

Shan sighed again. "I really like him, Al."

"It sounds like it," I replied.

"I think he wants a Frisbee," Shan hissed into the phone.

"A Frisbee?" I said, confused. "What for? And why are you whispering about it?"

"Kiss me," Shan said, a little louder. "Not a Frisbee. I think he wants to *kiss* me."

"How do you know?" I asked.

"It's the way he looks at me when he says good night," she said. "I can't explain it. I just think he does."

"Then why doesn't he?"

"I don't know," said Shan. "I think maybe he's never done it before, either."

I didn't know what to say. I wanted to give her some great best friend advice that would be really helpful. But part of me was jealous. She was apparently way ahead of me on the whole kissing thing. I'd always thought it would happen to us at the same time. I mean, we'd done all the big things together. We'd gotten our ears pierced together. We'd bought our first bras together. We'd even gotten our first periods within the same month. I'd just always figured we'd do everything together. But, apparently, Shan was doing this without me.

"Are you okay?" Shan asked me. I realized I hadn't said anything for a long time.

"Yeah," I said. "I, um, thought I heard my mother calling me."

"I e-mailed you a picture of me and Hector," said Shan, thankfully not picking up on the fact that I had just totally lied to her. "His brother took it with his digital camera. Let me know what you think."

"I will," I promised. "I should go now."

"Okay," said Shan. "I'll call you later."

I hung up. I went to the computer on my desk and opened my e-mail program. Sure enough, there was one from Shan. I opened it and read her note: "Me and my boyfriend!" was all it said. I clicked on the attached file, and a picture opened up. It was Shan standing next to a guy with dark hair and glasses. They were both wearing T-shirts that said San Francisco on them, and they were standing on a hill. Behind them was the Golden Gate Bridge. Hector had his arm around Shan, and she was grinning goofily.

"He's cute," I said out loud. "Congratulations."

I closed the picture and sighed. Hector *was* cute, and he and Shan looked really happy together. I decided I had to do something. I was tired of feeling like a loser. I was tired of Megan always showing me up and trying to make me feel bad (which, apparently, was working). It was time to make a change and become a new Allie, one who didn't wait around for boys to ask her out.

What this boiled down to is that I decided that I *would* ask Jack out. In fact, I was determined. I knew it was crazy. After all, he seemed to be totally into Megan, who knows why. Still, I was going to try. It was part of my whole new philosophy. Okay, so I didn't really have a whole new philosophy. But it was a start.

I decided that I would call him the next day.

As it turned out, I didn't have to wait until after work on Monday, because Jack came into the shop Monday morning with Barkley. Needless to say, as soon as I saw him, my whole calm-and-cool plan went right out the window. Instead, I went for surprised-and-uncool, which, I can say with total confidence, I pulled off to perfection.

"Uh," I said brightly, staring at Jack and forgetting everything I'd planned on saying.

He'd gotten a haircut over the weekend, and he looked adorable. He was also wearing a tanktop, which totally showed off his arms and chest. Never having seen him in anything besides baggy T-shirts, I hadn't realized how good a body he had. Really strong arms.

"Do you have time to give Barkley a nail trim?" he asked me. "He clicks on the hardwood floors when he walks, and it's making my mom nuts."

"Sure," I said. "Just give me a minute." *A minute to get over how utterly hot you are,* I thought silently.

"No problem," said Jack.

I slipped into the back room, so that Jack couldn't see me. *This is your chance!* my mind was screaming. Looking in the mirror, I saw immediately that my hair was a total mess. I pulled out my ponytail and quickly shook out my hair. It looked a little bit better, but still didn't help the zit on my chin or hide the fact that I had dirt on my face where one of the dogs had jumped up on me that morning. But it was now or never.

I closed my eyes and tried to breathe. *It's okay,* I said, giving myself a little pep talk. *You can do this. He's just a boy.*

I opened my eyes, hoping that some miracle might have occurred and I would look gorgeous. But no, I still looked like me. I wiped the mud off my cheek with my sleeve. Then I returned to the main room, trying to sound more positive than I felt. "Okay, then," I said. "Who's ready for a nail trim?"

Barkley wagged his stub of a tail at me as I knelt and gently picked him up, one hand under his chest and one around his back legs.

"Do you need help with that?" asked Jack.

"No," I said. "I'm fine, thanks." I was hoping he'd be impressed by how smoothly I'd picked Barkley up.

Barkley sat down on the table and watched as I picked up the nail clippers. He wasn't at all nervous, which was a really good thing, because I was. I'd trimmed toenails a million times, but suddenly I felt like it was the first time I'd ever held a dog's paw. I knew Jack was watching, and I wanted him to be impressed, especially since every time he'd seen me with dogs before, I'd managed to do something dumb.

"Good boy," I told Barkley as I lifted his right paw. Slipping the first nail into the clipper, I pinched the handles. A tiny piece of nail fell to the table with a little "click."

"So, how's it been around here?" Jack asked as I worked.

"Great," I said. "I've been really busy. How about you?"

"Oh, you know," he said. "I've been pretty busy, too. I volunteer at the shelter three days a week."

Yeah, I thought as I worked on Barkley's toes, *and on the other two you take out Megan.*

"And then there's the club committee," Jack continued.

"Right," I said as I cut another of Barkley's toenails, finishing the right paw. "That's *so* much fun." I hadn't meant to sound sarcastic, but it just slipped out. I hoped Jack wouldn't notice, as I was trying to make him see that I was a nice person.

"It's something, all right," Jack said. "Megan sure knows what she wants."

What she wants is you, I wanted to say.

"Who are you going with to the Fourth of July party?" asked Jack as I started on Barkley's left paw.

"Oh, nobody," I answered, surprised by his question. "It's not really that kind of thing." As soon as I said it, I realized what a mistake I'd made. It had been the perfect opportunity to ask Jack out, and I'd blown it.

"Oh," he said before I could correct myself. "Megan said everyone comes with a date."

Oh. *Great.* I had a sinking feeling I knew

where the conversation was headed. Then, as I was working up the nerve to speak again, the door opened.

"There you are," said Megan. "I've been looking for you."

I couldn't believe it. Did Megan have some kind of tracker on Jack, so that she always knew where he was? He was like one of those sharks they tag on the Nature Channel and then follow everywhere to see what it's doing. Every time Jack came around me, Megan managed to ruin everything.

"Well, here I am," Jack said.

"I'm going to leave Tallulah here for the afternoon," Megan announced.

I didn't turn around. "Just put her out back," I said.

Megan sniffed. "How can you watch her if she's out there?" she said. "I wouldn't want anything to happen to my little girl. I mean, look what happened at the park the other day."

I didn't say anything. Megan huffed, then turned and walked toward the back door. When she was out of earshot, Jack said, "I tried to tell her it was all Tallulah's fault," he said. "But you know how she is."

"Yeah," I said. *So,* I thought, *he* was *the one who told Megan about what happened.*

"It *was* kind of funny," Jack said, laughing a little.

I felt myself bristle. Was he making fun of me? Again? It sure sounded like it. If he was, he was bordering on jerkboy territory again, and this time, I wasn't sure I could let it go without saying something.

"Are you sure that yard is safe?" Megan sounded worried, as if she'd walked into the back and found a tar pit in the middle of it. "The fence doesn't look that sturdy."

"It's *fine*," I said. "As long as someone doesn't dig her way *under* it."

Megan didn't get the jab. She did, however, have one of her own to throw my way. "It's funny how bad things seem to happen around you, Allie," she said. "It's like you're cursed or something. Remember that time in fourth grade when we sang 'The Twelve Days of

Christmas' at the Christmas concert?"

I knew what she was about to do, but I couldn't stop her. I could only listen as she said to Jack, "It was *so* funny. On the last verse, we each had our own line to sing. Mine was five golden rings. Allie's was seven swans a swimming. Only she forgot the words, and instead of saying 'seven swans a swimming,' she said 'seven spiders spinning.' It was hysterical."

Megan laughed loudly. Then I heard Jack laugh, too, and it was like having the wind knocked out of me. I couldn't breathe. I felt my heart pounding in my chest. Everything seemed to stop, and all I heard was laughter in my head.

Then I heard Barkley yelp. I shook my head and looked down. A big piece of toenail was lying on the table, and there was a spot of blood on my hand. I'd cut his nail too short.

"Oh, Barkley," I said, reaching for a towel. "I'm so sorry, sweetie."

Barkley wagged his tail, but I knew it must have hurt him. I patted his nail and opened the can of powder we use to stop the bleeding. It's really easy to cut a dog's nail too short, especially when they're black, like Barkley's. Still, I felt awful. He was such a nice dog, and hurting him, even by mistake, upset me. As I put the powder on his nail, he bent his head and licked my hand, as if he was telling me it was okay.

"Look at all that blood," said Megan. Her tone made it sound as if she'd walked into the middle of a crime scene. "I think I might be sick."

Jack came over and rubbed Barkley's ears. "You okay, fella?" he asked.

"I'm so sorry," I told him.

"It's okay," Jack said. "I don't think he'll be crippled for life or anything." He was so close that I could smell the soap he'd used to shower with. He smelled like a pine forest.

"Is he all right?" Megan called out.

"He's fine," Jack told her, moving away from me and taking the forest smell with him.

"Thank heavens," said Megan. "I mean, he cried so loud, I thought maybe his foot was broken or something."

Carefully, I trimmed the last of Barkley's nails. Jack helped him off the table, and Barkley shook himself.

"Good as new," Jack said.

I nodded, not looking at him.

"What do I owe you?" asked Jack.

"It should be *free*," said Megan. "After all that."

"It's okay," I said to Jack. "We're good."

He looked at me for a moment, his brown eyes staring into mine. Some pieces of hair were hanging over his forehead, and I almost reached up and brushed them into place. Then Jack stepped back.

"Okay then," he said. "Thanks."

"Want to come over to my house?" asked Megan, apparently forgetting how "upset" she'd been about Barkley just a second before. "We could watch a DVD or something."

"I've got to get to the shelter," Jack said. "Maybe later."

"Oh," said Megan. "Well, I'll walk with you

back to your house."

Jack waved to me, and he and Megan left. I looked down at the spot of blood on the table. "He cried so loud," I said, imitating Megan's voice. "I thought maybe his foot was broken."

I wiped the blood away with the towel, then sprayed the top with antibacterial soap. As I scrubbed it, I fumed over the total disaster my brilliant plan had become. Not only hadn't I asked Jack out, but I'd hurt his dog *and*, thanks once again to Megan, had another of my embarrassing Regrettable Incidents shared with him.

It was true about the stupid swans. I had sung "seven spiders spinning" instead. I'd been so excited about the concert, I'd practiced my one line for weeks. Then when my big moment came, I totally blanked. So when I opened my mouth, "seven spiders spinning" came out instead.

It felt like everyone in the auditorium laughed. Standing on stage, I could hear them roaring. And for weeks afterward, kids teased me about it. Someone even left seven plastic spiders in my desk one day, and I had a pretty good idea who it was.

And now, thanks to her, Jack had laughed at me too. So much for thinking I'd actually ask him out. That was the biggest laugh of all.

Chapter Thirteen

The second meeting of the Fourth of July party committee met on Wednesday. I don't know why I even bothered to go — I guess I was just too proud to quit. I didn't want Megan to think she'd succeeded in scaring me off. Thankfully, it wasn't at Megan's house this time. Instead, we had it at the country club, in the game room. At least there I felt like we were on neutral territory, even if Megan had the Megbots on her side.

Also, there were boys. Without a baseball game to save them from the horrors of party planning, the guys showed up, reluctantly, to help out. As soon as they walked in, the Megbots descended on them like vultures on roadkill. I almost felt sorry for the guys, except that I was still on my Not Caring About Boys and the Stupid Girls They Talk To campaign.

Of course Jack was there. Megan latched on to him the minute he arrived, which was fine with me. As long as he stayed away from me, I could not-like him without a problem. All I had to do was look at him and Megan, think about them laughing at me, and I'd remember why I don't like him.

"Tonight is all about decorations," Megan said once everyone was there. "We decided to do bouquets of red, white, and blue flowers. We can't afford real ones, so we're using these cool paper ones that Amber's mom found at Pier 1. Aren't they great?"

Everyone oohed and aahed as Megan poured a bunch of fake flowers out on the table. "And we have this ribbon to tie them up with," she added, producing three rolls in colors that matched the flowers. "All we have to do is take some flowers and tie them together. Like this."

She took some flowers of each color, held them together, and demonstrated tying them in a bow.

"Okay," she said, holding her bouquet up like it was an Academy Award or something. "Let's get busy."

It turned out that Megan's idea of "getting busy" was to go sit on the couch on the other side of the room with the Megbots to do something that wasn't making bouquets. With the girls gone, the boys lost interest and started talking about sports and whatever else boys talk about together. I really wasn't listening.

I picked up some flowers, cut a length of ribbon, and tied up my first bouquet.

"Nice work."

Jack sat down next to me. I didn't say anything as he picked up some flowers and tried to tie them together. His bow was a mess, though, and he held the bouquet in his hands, staring at it with a funny expression. He looked so helpless that I forgot for a moment that I was not-liking him.

"You didn't tie it right," I said. "Here." I took the bouquet from him and showed him how to tie the ribbon so that the bow was neat.

"Got it," he said. As he took it back from my hand, our fingers touched, like they had that first time when he'd handed me back Rufus's leash. I pulled my hand away and went back to work on my own bouquets. I was mad at myself for even talking to him, but it wasn't like I really had a choice. I couldn't just sit there like a statue all night.

"How's Barkley?" I asked him.

"Fine," said Jack. "It really wasn't a big deal, you know."

I shrugged. "Not to you," I told him. "But it wasn't your paw."

Jack smiled. I still wasn't looking at him, but out of the corner of my eye I saw him push the hair out of his eyes. I couldn't help it—my heart fluttered a little.

"They're really into this whole patriotic thing, aren't they?" Jack remarked, starting on a new bouquet.

"I'm not sure they're actually into it at all,"

I said, glancing over at Megan and her friends. "They haven't done any of the work."

"I noticed that," said Jack. "I sort of thought this would be more of a team effort."

"Only if you're on their team," I said.

"I take it you're not," Jack said.

I snorted. "Hardly," I told him. "I'm afraid I'm not quite up to their standards."

Jack laughed. "I think you're on a team all your own," he told me.

I didn't know what he meant by that. Was he teasing me again? Did he mean I was *better* than Megan and the Megbots, or that I was just *weirder* than they were? He didn't elaborate, and I wasn't about to ask him. I'd already broken my promise to myself not to talk to him. I wasn't going to give him the satisfaction of thinking I cared what he thought of me.

"Look at you two, all busy and everything."

Megan was standing behind us, eyeing the bouquets Jack and I had made. "You're just like Santa's little elves or something," she said, putting her hand on Jack's shoulder and giving it a squeeze.

"Just like," I said.

"Let me help you," Megan said sweetly, taking the seat on Jack's other side. "Girls, come on!" she called out to the Megbots.

Suddenly I was surrounded by Megbots. They all talked at once, and the subject was themselves. Specifically, they discussed what they were going to wear to the party.

"I found the *perfect* dress," Megan announced, tossing a badly made bouquet on the table and reaching for some more flowers. "It's white, strapless, and *really* gorgeous. I saw it at The Limited. My mother's taking me to the mall tomorrow night to get it."

"It sounds perfect," one of the Megbots said.

"It is," said Megan proudly, like she'd made the dress herself.

They continued talking about clothes, and shoes, and how they were going to wear their hair. I tuned them out until they were nothing but static in the background. I concentrated on making bouquets, one after the other, until there was a huge pile in front of me. The Megbots each had four or five, while I had three dozen. The boys had maybe three between them, with the exception of Jack, who had made seven.

I decided that I'd made enough, and got up to take a break. As I walked away from the table, I heard Megan say, "Some people just don't want to do their share."

I ignored her and went over to the soda machine that stood beside the ping-pong tables. I fished in my pocket for some quarters, dropped them in, and hit one of the buttons. When the can of soda rolled out, I picked it up and flipped the top.

To my surprise, Jack had followed me. "Root beer," he said, looking at the can in my hand. "No diet 7-Up? It seems to be the drink of choice over there."

"What can I say?" I told him. "I'm a rebel."

He put his money in and chose a Cherry Coke. "Me too," he said as he took his soda and opened it.

I walked over to an armchair and sat down. Again, Jack followed me, taking a seat in the chair across from me. I wished he would just let me be by myself, especially if he was going to make fun of me again. But I was also kind of happy that he'd followed me. Correction—I was happy that he'd left Megan and come after me.

"So, you find anyone to go to the party with yet?" he asked.

I shook my head. "Haven't looked," I said. I wondered why he was asking. Was *he* thinking of asking me? The thought suddenly occurred to me, and almost instantly I felt my palms start to get sweaty. I'd just assumed that he was going with Megan. But maybe I was wrong. Maybe . . . I couldn't even let myself think about it.

Jack took a sip of his Coke, but didn't say anything. I noticed his leg was kind of bouncing up and down, like he was nervous about something. He took another drink and cleared his throat. I'd never seen him act that way. He'd always been so cool, like he wasn't afraid of anything.

"Can I ask you something?" he said.

I looked over at him. Was this it? I felt my heart begin to race as I nodded at him. "Sure,"

I said, trying to sound casual.

"I was just wondering —," he started.

Yes! I shouted in my head, even before he'd finished the sentence. *Yes, I'll go to the party with you.*

"Jack!"

Megan was standing up at the table and looking over at us. "Get back over here," Megan said. "We have to make a bunch more of these."

Jack looked back at me. He opened his mouth, and I waited to hear him ask me out. Instead he said, "We should probably go. She won't stop yelling until we do."

He stood up. I waited a few seconds, hoping what had just happened hadn't actually happened, then got up and followed him back to the table. I knew Megan didn't care whether I came back to help or not — and apparently Jack didn't either — but making bouquets beat sitting in a chair thinking about how Jack had just not-asked me out.

"I was just telling the girls that a rose corsage would look great with my dress," Megan said to Jack. "They have those blue roses now, so it could be in all three colors."

The Megbots giggled. I knew full well what Megan was getting at with her "hint" to Jack. She was going to get him to be her date for the party if it was the last thing she did. And I couldn't think of any reason why she wouldn't get exactly what she wanted. She always did.

"I think I'm going to wear my hair up," I heard Megan say.

Again I retreated into my own private world. There was no Megan there, no Megbots, no Jack. I was all by myself. My pimply-chinned, boring-haired, never-been-kissed self.

Suddenly, I stood up. "I've got to go," I said. I couldn't stand sitting there another minute with Megan making her play for Jack, and Jack totally not seeing how awful she was. Okay, so it was more about being upset that Jack wasn't seeing how much better *I* was for him than Megan, but I couldn't let myself admit that right then. It would have hurt too much.

I left as quickly as I could, knowing that everyone was watching me. I didn't stop until I was on the club's front steps. Then I called my dad on my cell phone and asked him to come get me.

While I waited for him to get there, I looked up at the sky. I could see the Little Dipper. Then I found Orion. Like I said before, my dad has taught me a lot about the stars. I even have a favorite constellation. It probably isn't much of a shock that it's Canis Major, the Big Dog. And my favorite star in Canis Major is Sirius, the Dog Star. It's the brightest star in the sky, even brighter than the sun. It takes something like eight years for the light from Sirius to reach Earth. That means that I was five years old when the light I was looking at now had started on its way through space. That's pretty amazing when you think about it.

Looking up at Canis Major, I did something I hadn't done since I was a kid. You know that old nursery rhyme about wishing on a star? That's what I did. I wished on the Dog Star. Only I can't tell you what I wished. Not yet. If I did, then it wouldn't come true.

Chapter Fourteen

Ugh, I thought as I looked at myself in the mirror. *I look like a wedding cake.*

I was at the mall looking for something to wear to the Fourth of July party. After being mad for the past twenty-four hours, I'd decided that not going to the party would make Megan happy. She'd think she'd gotten Jack *and* chased me away. And I wasn't about to give her the satisfaction. She might have Jack, but I could still show up and have a good time. Besides, I really did want to see the fireworks and everything. There was no reason something as dumb as a guy should get in the way of that.

So far, though, I wasn't having any luck. I took the dress off and hung it up alongside the four other dresses I'd tried on. None of them looked right. They either made me look like I had the biggest butt in the world or, like the wedding cake dress, there was way too much going on with bows and ruffles and stuff.

Why, I wondered, didn't they make dresses for girls with *normal* bodies?

And it wasn't just my body; it was everything. My hair was pulled back in a ponytail, which I liked because it kept it out of my face. But it was so blah-looking. And I don't like fussing around with makeup either. I mean, who has time? Besides, Shan swears that makeup gives you major zits, and I was already starting to get another one on my chin. I poked at it, even though I know that's the perfect way to make a pimple become ginormous.

Besides the hair and face, there were my nails, which were cut really short because you can't have long nails when you work with dogs. And my clothes, well, let's just say I dress to be comfortable, not to impress anyone.

I left the dressing room and tried to find something else. As I pawed through the racks of dresses, I wondered if Megan spent as much time not-liking me as I did not-liking her. She sure seemed to put a lot of effort into making me feel bad. But why? I didn't see what she got out of it. She was already basically the most popular girl in our class. The Megbots thought she was the Queen of Everything. Why did she have it in for me, who wasn't the queen of anything? I didn't get it.

I gave up on the store and walked out empty-handed. It seemed like it was going to be a useless trip. There was no dress in the world that was going to make me feel better about going to the party.

I fully intended to go straight home, but as I passed by the window of The Limited, something caught my eye. One of the mannequins inside was wearing a white dress. I stopped and looked at it. *White*, I thought. *Strapless*.

I knew immediately that it was *the* dress. Megan's dress. The most perfect dress in the world. The one she had spent most of the night before talking about.

She'd been right about one thing—it *was* gorgeous. To make matters worse, I knew just how she'd look in it, and that made me jealous. Looking at it, I had to admit that I would give anything to look good in a dress like that.

Why don't you try it on? said a voice in my head. A slightly evil voice.

It was a stupid idea, I knew. The dress wouldn't look right on me. I just wasn't the glamorous type. I wasn't Megan with her skinny legs and blond hair.

Go on, the voice prodded me. *It can't hurt.*

I hesitated another moment, then walked into the shop and headed for the dress rack. I found the white dress. There was only one left in my size. Before I could talk myself out of it, I took it into a dressing room. A minute later I was looking at myself in the mirror.

I was shocked. The dress actually looked okay. No, it looked better than okay. It was beautiful. Even with my boring hair and short nails it made me look, well, almost pretty. I couldn't believe it. Me. Pretty.

Buy it! screamed that desperate voice in my head.

I looked at the price tag attached to the dress. It was expensive. *Really* expensive. I don't think most of the clothes in my closet added together cost as much as that dress. It was way more than I'd planned on spending. There was no way I could buy it. I started to take it off.

Megan would die *if she saw you in this,* said the voice.

I stopped and looked at myself again. I imagined Megan rushing into the store, all set to plunk down her mother's credit card, then seeing that her dress was gone. Then I pictured her face when I walked into the party wearing *her* dress. She *would* die. I was sure of it. And thinking about that made me strangely happy.

But it was so expensive. I looked at the price tag again. The thought of spending that much money on a dress made me sick. Then I thought about Megan again. First she'd be mad when she couldn't wear the dress she wanted.

Then she'd see *me* in it at the party.

And Jack would see you in it too, the voice said.

I took the dress off in a hurry and put my own clothes back on. I had to have it. Yes, it was expensive. But I had the money I'd earned from working at Perfect Paws. It was enough to buy the dress. I would have to spend almost all of it, though. Was it worth it?

It was. This wasn't just about making Megan miserable. This was about finally having my own chance to be the beautiful one — the *winner.*

I took the dress to the register and set it down. The woman behind the counter picked it up. "Good choice," she said. "It's a stunning dress. What's the special occasion?"

Ruining Megan Fitzmartin's life and making Jack McKenna fall in love with me, I wanted to say. Instead, I smiled and answered, "A party."

"Well, you'll be the prettiest girl there," the woman said as she rang up the dress. When she told me the final cost, I handed her practically all my money.

The saleswoman put the dress in a fancy

dress bag and gave it to me. "Have fun," she said.

"I will," I told her.

I took the bus home. The whole way, I thought about how I was going to show Megan up. I imagined every detail, from the shocked look on her face when she saw me to the way I was going to look at her, say, "Nice dress," and turn my back on her so she could see me walking away in the dress she really wanted. It made me feel good. A little queasy, maybe, but excited nevertheless.

Back at home, I took the dress out of the bag and hung it on the back of my bedroom door. I lay on my bed and just looked at it. And the longer I looked at it, the less happy I got. I know. I know. I said how excited I was about getting Megan's dress. And I was. For a while. But the longer I stared at that dress, the more I realized that I wasn't really showing her up; I was behaving exactly like she would.

It had all seemed like such a good idea at the time. And if I were a different kind of person—a person like Megan or any of the Megbots—I probably would have never felt bad about doing it. But I wasn't like them.

I knew what I had to do. I had to take the dress back. As much as I hated to do it, I had to return it. I got up and started to put it back in the bag. Just then, though, I heard my mother calling me from downstairs to come help her with dinner. I'd have to return the dress the next day. Running my hands over the silky fabric, I gave the dress one last look before going downstairs.

Chapter Fifteen

The next morning, I put the dress back in its bag and took it with me to the shop. I hung it on the back of a chair in the storeroom where we keep the shampoo and put a towel over it so that my mother wouldn't see it. I knew that if she did, she'd see how beautiful it was and make me keep it. And I couldn't tell her that I'd only gotten it because I didn't want Megan to have it.

I only had two dogs signed up for day care that day. Because of the Fourth of July weekend, a lot of people were going out of town and taking their dogs with them. Only Walter and Wendell were coming in, and just for baths. I was actually happy to have so little to do. It gave me time to organize the shop, which I hadn't done for a while.

Then, like a dark cloud rolling over the perfect summer sky, Megan came in with Tallulah. When I saw her I got incredibly nervous. I looked around, thinking for some reason that I'd left the dress lying around in plain sight. But it was safe in its bag in the other room.

Megan looked mad. She stormed up to the counter. "I'm leaving her here," she said, handing me Tallulah's leash.

"For how long?" I asked, hoping my voice sounded normal. I was terrified that Megan would use her powers of evil to figure out what I was up to.

"I don't know," Megan snapped. "I have to go look for a dress for the party."

I felt myself turning red. "Oh?" I said. "What about the one you liked so much?"

"Someone else got it," she answered. "I went to pick it up last night and it was gone. I looked *everywhere* in that store for it. I even had them call the store over in Brixton. They didn't have one in my size either." She looked at me. "I can't believe someone else would buy *my* dress," she said, apparently forgetting for a minute that she and I weren't friends and that, normally, I wouldn't care anything about her dress problem.

"That's too bad," I said.

"Now I have to go find another one," she said. "I'm so mad. Why does everything happen to me?"

I was hoping she would leave soon. Knowing that her dress was in the other room, I was getting more and more nervous. I don't know how criminals can lie. I'm terrible at it. I was convinced that it was totally obvious that I was the one who had stolen Megan's dress out from under her.

Then I had another realization. If Megan went shopping before I could return her dress, she still wouldn't be able to get it. Then, even if I did return it, I'd still feel bad. It was stupid, I know, but I couldn't help it. After all, I was going through a lot of trouble to *not* be like her. If in the end she didn't get the dress she wanted, then it would basically be like I'd kept it.

"You know," I said, thinking fast. "You might want to check the store again later today."

"Why would I do that?" asked Megan, as if it was the stupidest suggestion ever.

"Well," I said. "Sometimes people get things home and decide they don't like them. Maybe whoever bought it will return it."

"You'd have to be an idiot to return that dress," Megan said. "It's perfect." She hesitated. "Still," she said. "I guess there's a chance."

I could see her mind working and hoped that for once she'd see things my way. My heart raced as I waited for her to say something.

"Yeah, maybe I'll check the store again this afternoon, just in case."

She didn't even thank me for the suggestion, which was no big shock. She just turned and walked out. I breathed a big sigh of relief. I still had time to get the dress back.

But only if I worked fast. I looked at the clock. If I left right then, I could get to the mall and return the dress in time for Megan to find it when she went back later in the day. Then I remembered the leash in my hand, and Tallulah on the other end of it. I couldn't just leave her at the shop. And I couldn't take her to the mall with me.

I could take her to my house, though. I'd left Rufus there, and although I hated to subject him to even an hour with Tallulah, I could put her in the yard with him, take the bus to the mall, come back and pick Tallulah up, and be back in the shop before my mother suspected anything. It was a perfect plan.

I told my mother I was taking Tallulah to the park. She was busy going over the receipts for the week and was a little distracted. "Have a nice time," she said as I grabbed the dress bag from the storeroom and hurried out.

"We have to hurry," I said to Tallulah as we walked toward my house.

Tallulah ignored me. She was too busy sniffing around some bushes. I stopped and let her smell. She was really sticking her head in the bush, like she had found something fascinating.

"Tallulah," I said, tugging on her leash. "Come on. Please?"

Tallulah gave a sharp bark as something burst from the bushes. It was a cat, a small orange-and-white tabby that took off down the sidewalk. Tallulah, barking like crazy, ran after it. Somehow she managed to wrap the leash around my legs. When she pulled, I stumbled. *Not again*, I thought as I felt the leash start to slip from my hand.

As the leash slid over my wrist, it caught on the dress bag. I watched in horror as Tallulah took off and the dress, caught in the leash, went with her. She followed the kitty as it ran down the street, the dress flapping behind her. I couldn't believe what was happening. I just stood there and watched, horrified, as the dress got dragged along the sidewalk.

Tallulah and the cat disappeared into a yard a few houses away. When I finally got my legs to move, I ran after them. Tallulah had lost sight of the cat and was running around the yard yapping. The dress was still attached to her leash, and now the bag had torn open. The dress was being dragged through the dirt.

I tried to catch Tallulah, but she kept darting just out of reach. With every step, her tiny paws pressed the dress deeper and deeper into the dirt.

"Stop it!" I shouted.

Tallulah, to my surprise, stopped barking and looked at me. She sat down, right on top of the dress, and stared at me, her mouth open. I swear it looked just like she was laughing.

I shooed Tallulah away from the dress and held it up. There were dirty paw prints all over it. Looking at it, I wanted to cry. There was no way I could return it now.

I couldn't believe what was happening. First I'd stolen Megan's dress. Then, when I tried to do the right thing and return it, I'd ruined it. Now there was no way I could make things right. I wadded up the dress, shoved it into what was left of the bag, and walked back to Perfect Paws. Tallulah walked in front of me, bouncing along like the happiest dog in the world.

"That was fast," my mother called out from her office when she heard me come in.

"Yeah," I said, quickly stuffing the dress underneath the front counter so she wouldn't see it. "Tallulah wasn't really into it."

When Megan came in that afternoon, she was in an even worse mood than she'd been in that morning. She had a bunch of bags in her hands, but her face was tight and angry-looking.

"Find anything?" I asked her.

She held up the bags and shook them, as if the answer should be obvious. "No one returned the dress," she said, like it was my fault. Which it was, but I couldn't tell her that. "I'm stuck with one of these. But I don't like any of them."

I didn't say anything. If I had still been operating under my original plan, I would have been thrilled to see her so unhappy. Instead, I felt guilty. Megan's dress was sitting in the bag under the counter, less than a foot away from her. But even if I'd wanted to, I couldn't give it to her. I'd ruined it. Well, Tallulah had ruined it, but it was the same thing.

Megan took Tallulah and left. For the rest of the day, I tried to think of some way to make things better. And I kept thinking, all through the weekend, which seemed to stretch on forever. I'd shoved the bag with the dress in it into my closet when I got home on Friday. I couldn't even look at it.

I was feeling terrible. I didn't want to, but I had to tell someone. Being all alone with my guilt was making me crazy. I needed someone to tell me what to do. I tried to call Shan, but no one answered at her grandparents' house. Finally, I went looking for my mother. I fully anticipated her being horrified at my behavior, but I couldn't think of anything else to do.

I found her in the bathroom. She was standing in front of the mirror, a bottle of something dark in her hand and a towel around her neck.

"What are you doing?" I asked her.

"Just touching up my roots," she answered, putting the tip of the bottle against her scalp and squeezing.

"You're dyeing your hair?" I said, surprised.

"I'm not dyeing it, exactly," she said. "Only the gray parts."

I stood in the doorway, watching her for a minute and trying to work up the courage to tell her about the dress. And that's when I got my Grand Idea.

Chapter Sixteen

On Monday morning, I arrived at Perfect Paws with the dress in my backpack. Also in there was a bottle of dye. I'd bought it at the drugstore on my way to the shop. Now all I needed was some time alone to do what I needed to do.

"Do you mind watching the store by yourself for a few hours?" my mother asked me when she saw I was there. "I need to go to the printer to okay the new design for our business cards, and then I thought I'd pick up another case of that all-natural flea soap. We're running low." It was like she'd read my mind.

"Sure," I told her, trying to sound casual. This was perfect. With her gone, I could dye the dress and have it hidden again before she came back.

"There are no appointments until one," she said. "I'll be back by then."

"Great," I said. With no responsibilities, I was totally free and clear to work on the dress.

As soon as my mother left, I took the dress out of the backpack. Then I read the directions on the back of the bottle of dye. It said to add the dye to a tubful of water and mix it well.

"No problem," I said. I could use one of the tubs we washed the dogs in.

I set the bottle beside a tub and turned on the water. As it filled up, I looked at the dress. Because it was white, I figured it would be no problem to dye it. I'd wiped a lot of the dirt off, and the remaining paw prints were light enough that I was pretty sure the dye would cover them. I'd picked a nice blue color. I would still be stuck with a dress I didn't want, but at least I could wear it. And with any luck, Megan wouldn't notice that it was the one she'd wanted.

I was about to pour the dye into the water when the door opened and someone came in. I looked out and saw Megan standing by the counter. *Now what?* I thought. Hurrying, I grabbed up the dress, wadded it into a ball, and stuffed it into the hamper we used for wet dog towels. Then I went to see what Megan wanted.

"Tallulah needs a bath," Megan said. "I want her to look beautiful for the party tomorrow."

"Okay," I said quickly. "I can do that."

"Fine," Megan said. "I'll be back in an hour."

I thought about the dress. If I took an hour to wash Tallulah, I wouldn't have much time to dye the dress before my mother got back. But if I hurried, I could just make it.

"That's perfect," I told Megan, taking Tallulah. "Bye."

I didn't wait for her answer. I carried Tallulah into the washroom. Since the sink was already filled with warm water, I put Tallulah in it. When her feet touched the water, she started scratching at the side of the tub, trying to get out.

"Stay still," I told her, attempting to hold her with one hand while I reached for the bottle of Snowy Kote shampoo that we use to get white dogs nice and clean.

Tallulah ignored me. She got more frantic, scratching and whining. Her little paws scrabbled against the sides of the tub, making an awful sound.

"Tallulah!" I said. "Come on. It's not that bad."

I almost had my fingers on the bottle. Then Tallulah jumped up, splashing me. I tried to cover my face, and when I did, I knocked over the bottle of dye. It all poured into the tub, turning the water a bright blue. I looked down in horror as Tallulah splashed around in the water, soaking herself.

"No!" I shrieked. "No, no, no, no, no." I tried to grab Tallulah, but her paws slipped and her head went under the water. When she came up, her face looked like she'd eaten a blueberry pie and gotten it all over her fur.

I picked Tallulah up and put her in another tub. I washed her with Snowy Kote, hoping it would remove the dye. It didn't. When I was done, she was still blue. All of her, from the tip of her snout to the tip of her tail. Looking at her, I wanted to laugh. But I was so upset, all I could do was fight back tears.

When Megan showed up an hour later, she took one look at blue Tallulah and let out a piercing scream. "What did you do to her?" she yelled, reaching down to pick up her dog, then pulling back, like maybe Tallulah was contagious or something.

"It's dye," I told her. "I'm really sorry. It was an accident. Don't worry. It will wear off."

"Wear off?" Megan shouted. "How long will that take?"

I honestly didn't know. "A couple of weeks?" I suggested. "A month or two?"

"A month or two?" Megan glared at me. "What about the party? It's *tomorrow*, in case you've forgotten. I can't take her to the club looking like this. Everyone will laugh at her."

I glanced at Tallulah, who was licking her blue paw. It looked like she was sucking on a Popsicle.

"At least she matches the color scheme," I said.

Megan made a sound like she was going to explode. She snatched Tallulah's leash from me. "You are *never* going to live this down," she said to me. "I can guarantee that."

She turned and stomped off, pulling Tallulah behind her. I couldn't do anything but watch them go. I raised my hand to rub my eyes, and that's when I noticed that my fingers were blue. I held up my other hand. It was blue too. The color stopped halfway to my elbows. I looked like I was wearing blue gloves.

"That's just great," I said. There was no way the dye was coming off. My mother was going to see it. Everyone was going to see it. My life was over.

I went back to the sink. The blue water was still sloshing around in the tub. I thought about trying to dye the dress after all, but what was the point? I wasn't going to wear it. Not after what had happened. Megan would take one look at it and know what I'd done. *I* would look at it and know what I'd done. Worst of all,

Jack would know what I'd done, because Megan would be sure to tell him.

I opened the drain and watched the blue water go down. Then I cleaned both the tubs. When I was done, my hands were still blue and the dress was still white with little brown paw prints. I sat down in a chair and put my head in my hands.

When my mother walked in, half an hour later, the first thing she said was, "Why are you wearing rubber gloves?"

I wiggled my fingers at her. "They're not gloves."

"What happened?" she said, sounding really worried. She came over and took one of my hands in hers, turning it over and back again like she'd never seen a hand before.

"It's a long story," I said. "I'm not sure I want to tell it. I don't come out looking so great."

"How bad can it be?" she said. "It's just a little dye." She looked at me strangely. "You weren't trying to dye your hair, were you?"

"I wish it was that," I said.

"Worse?" asked my mother, like there was no possible way it could be.

"Way worse," I said.

I told her the whole story, even showing her the dress. She looked at the paw prints and sighed. "It really was a beautiful dress," she said. She held it up in front of me. "Oh, and I bet you looked gorgeous in it."

"I did," I said. "Thanks for reminding me."

"I'm sorry," she said, folding the dress up and setting it down. "I know how you must feel."

"I doubt it," I told her. "I bet you never dyed your arms blue trying to cover up the stains you got on a dress you stole out from under the nose of a girl you wanted to get payback on because she was all over this guy you weren't even sure was worth liking."

"When you put it that way, well, no," my mother said. "But I think I have some idea. And like you told Megan, it will wear off."

"Not before tomorrow night," I said.

Chapter Seventeen

I picked up the phone and dialed Shan's grandparents' number. It rang seven times, and I was about to hang up when an old-sounding voice said, "Hello?"

"Hi," I said. "Is Shan there? This is her friend Allie."

"Allie," the voice said, sounding really happy that I'd called. "Shan talks about you all the time. This is her grandfather."

"Hi, Mr. Chan," I said.

"Shan tells us all the funny things you do," he said.

I had no idea what these funny things were, but I was sure going to ask Shan when I got to talk to her. "Shan says she's having a great time," I told him.

"Yes," said Mr. Chan. "Next time I hope you will come with her."

"That would be great," I said. "So, is Shan there?"

"No," he said. "She is at the movies. With her friend. The boy from down the street. I forget his name."

"Hector," I heard another voice, a woman's, call out.

"Yes, yes," Mr. Chan said. "Hector. She is out with Hector. At the movies," he repeated, I guess in case I'd forgotten in the past five seconds.

"Okay," I said. "Well, could you please tell her I called?"

"I will," Mr. Chan said. "Bye-bye."

I said good-bye and hung up. I really wanted to talk to Shan. Besides my mom, she was the only other person who would understand the utter calamity of my life. But I couldn't talk to her because she was too busy with Hector. Hector. Her friend the boy, as Mr. Chan would say. But I knew he wasn't a friendboy. He was her boyfriend. Shan had a boyfriend, and what did I have? Blue hands and a ruined dress.

I flipped over onto my stomach and pressed my face against a pillow. It was all stuffy, and I couldn't breathe. I wondered, briefly, if I could suffocate myself that way. Probably, I thought, I'd just pass out and humiliate myself some more by falling off the bed. I pictured the paramedics carrying me out of the house, one of them looking at the other and saying, "What's with her blue arms?"

I turned over onto my back, just in case. Why, I wondered, was I so completely hopeless? Why did so many bad things happen to *me*? Why couldn't they happen to Megan, or to one of the Megbots? I felt like I was Sleeping Beauty and my parents had forgotten to invite the evil fairy to my christening. Now her curse was upon me. Only instead of falling asleep, I was doomed to complete social failure.

Frankly, I think good old Beauty got off

pretty easy. I mean, how hard is it to *sleep*? All she had to do was lie there until a handsome prince came and kissed her. Then they threw her a big party and she got to live happily ever after. *She* never had to worry about a stupid Fourth of July party. *She* never had to listen to Megan and the Megbots laughing at her. *She* never had to wonder if the prince liked her. She just had to take a really long nap.

Maybe that was it, I thought. Maybe I was asleep and my entire life was one big nightmare. Maybe all I needed was for a handsome prince to come along and kiss me. Then I would wake up with perfect hair, perfect nails, a perfect dress, and a perfect boyfriend. We'd get on our horses and ride off to our castle, where every day little cartoon birds would bring us food and sing for us.

Right. No prince was ever going to kiss me. No *boy* was ever going to kiss me. I was highly unkissable. Especially now that I was semi-blue. What kind of guy wants to go out with a blue girl?

I closed my eyes and pretended I was

Sleeping Beauty. I imagined feeling someone's lips on mine. Then, weirdly enough, I did feel something. I felt something wet on my mouth, and hot breath on my face. I opened my eyes.

Rufus was standing next to the bed, looking at me with a worried expression. When he saw me open my eyes, he started wagging his tail. I patted the bed and he jumped up next to me and settled down, curling into a big ball with his back against my side. I leaned my head on his neck and put my arm around him.

"You're better than some stupid old prince," I told him.

He grunted, stretching his paws. I buried my face in his fur, which, I have to admit, didn't smell so great. "Ooh, Roof," I said. "Someone's getting a bath tomorrow."

Tomorrow. Tomorrow was the Fourth of July. I knew my parents were excited about going to the celebration at the country club. My father had been talking all week about the fireworks that the Fire Department was going to set off. And my mother had made her special strawberry angel food cake, which she said was *sure* to be better than anything anyone else brought.

Normally, I would have been kind of excited about July Fourth. It's a little corny, but I like fireworks and all that stuff. Plus, there were going to be lots of dogs there. But I couldn't get into this Fourth of July at all. Not one bit. All I wanted to do was stay home and not see anyone.

"Just you and me, Rufus," I said. "Why can't it just be you and me, together forever?"

Rufus didn't answer. He was sleeping, his big paws twitching as he dreamed about something, probably chasing squirrels. He let out a little bark. I rubbed his ears. "It's all right," I told him. "Everything's okay."

He quieted down, giving a deep sigh and settling back into sleep. I kissed him on top of his head. He was my big, stinky prince.

I picked up *Pride & Prejudice* and started reading. I was almost done with it, and was getting to the part where Mr. Darcy and Elizabeth finally—*finally*—tell each other how they feel. It was totally romantic, but it also made me even more depressed, so after a while I put the book down and closed my eyes.

I dreamed I was in a castle tower. I was lying on a big bed, wearing a pretty dress. I was asleep. I don't know how I knew that, since I was asleep and all, but I did. It was like I was watching a movie that I was starring in. I saw everything from the outside. I saw the moon through the tower window, round and full. I saw vines covered in thorns coming over the windowsill.

Suddenly, a face appeared in the window. It was Jack, only he was dressed like a prince in a fairy tale. He had climbed up the thorny vines. Now he pulled himself over the windowsill and walked slowly toward the bed I was on.

I watched him bend down and look at my face. He stared at it for a long time, as if I was the most beautiful thing he had ever seen, as if he'd slayed a hundred dragons and ridden a thousand miles searching for me because he was so in love with me. Then, in slow motion, he leaned down. He closed his eyes and parted his lips. He was going to kiss me.

"Cut!" someone shouted. Jack stood up. I opened my eyes, wondering why he hadn't kissed me, and who had yelled.

"That's not the way the story goes," said Megan, appearing from the shadows. "You don't kiss *her*," she told Jack. "She's the ugly stepsister. *I'm* the one you kiss."

As I watched, Megan put her arms around Jack. She started to kiss him. I heard myself scream, "No!"

I woke up. For a few seconds I had no idea where I was. Everything looked strange. Then I realized that it was because everything was dark. I was in my room. The moon was shining in through the window. Rufus was still next to me, snoring. I looked at the clock on my bedside table. It was one thirty in the morning.

I lay back down. I tried to sleep, but every time I closed my eyes I saw Megan kissing Jack. I tossed and turned, trying to get comfortable, but the sheets felt hot and sticky, like vines holding me down. Eventually I fell into a sort of half sleep, where it felt like I woke up every three minutes and never really rested.

The whole time, I heard Megan's voice whispering in my ear. "*I'm* the one he wants to kiss," she said. "Not you. Me." Over and over she said it, until it became a singsong rhyme I couldn't stop hearing: "*I'm* the one he wants to kiss. *I'm* the one he wants to kiss. *I'm* the one he wants to kiss."

When I woke up again, it was morning. Rufus was gone, and the sheets were twined around my legs. I was totally exhausted, as if I hadn't slept at all. I heard someone walking down the hall, and then my father stuck his head into my room.

"Good morning," he said, sounding way too happy.

"No, it's not," I said grumpily.

"Come on," he said. "We're going to have a ton of fun today. Get up and come downstairs. I'm making blueberry pancakes."

"Okay," I told him, just to make him go away.

When he was gone, I sat up. My head was pounding and my mouth tasted like I'd been sucking on dirty socks. "Blueberry pancakes," I said, looking at my blue hands. "How completely, exactly what I do *not* need right now."

I forced myself to stand up. As I walked out of my room I caught a glimpse of myself in the mirror. "Megan's right," I told myself as I started downstairs, where the smell of blueberries floated up from the kitchen, making me sick, "you *are* the ugly stepsister."

Chapter Eighteen

I tried to get out of going. I really did. At breakfast I coughed a little bit and sniffled, hoping my parents would notice and ask if I was getting a cold. They didn't. Then I decided just not to say anything at all, thinking maybe there was a chance they would somehow forget about the whole thing. I know. Fat chance. But short of faking a heart attack, I didn't know what else to do.

After breakfast, I went and hid in my room. I considered running away, at least long enough for my parents to leave without me. I even started to write a note telling them not to worry, that I'd be back later, after it was all over. But I'd barely written "Dear Mom and Dad" when there was a knock on my door.

"Come in," I said, shutting my notebook and trying to look like I wasn't up to anything.

My mother came in. "You're doing homework on a holiday?" she asked, looking suspiciously at my notebook.

"Writing a letter," I said.

"Mmm," my mother said. "Well, I was wondering if you want to go shopping."

"What for?" I asked.

"A dress," she answered. "For today."

I groaned. Looking at dresses was the last thing I wanted to do. "Do I have to?" I said.

"No," said my mother.

I looked up at her, totally shocked. "What?"

"You don't have to," she said. "You're old enough to make your own decision about it."

I was about to give her my answer, which was fully obvious to me, when she held up a finger. "But," she said, "I want you to consider what not going means."

"What does it mean?" I asked, not wanting to hear the answer.

"It means Megan and the Megbots win," she said.

It was funny to hear her use another Shanword. But I didn't laugh.

"That's so not fair," I said. See, she was right. If I didn't go to the Fourth of July party, then Megan would think I was afraid of her, or at least embarrassed. And I sort of was embarrassed. But I also wanted to show her that she couldn't scare me away.

"Who said anything about fair?" said my mom, looking at my face and knowing she'd said the one thing that would get me to change my mind about going.

"Okay," I said. "I'll go. But if this is a total disaster, you're going to owe me big-time."

"Deal," she said. "Now let's go. We don't have a lot of time."

We went back to the mall. Only it was more like launching a raid on an enemy fortress. My mother was a woman on a mission, charging through stores and looking through racks of dresses like there was a secret code hidden in one of them and we had to find it before the missile launched and wiped out Europe. Finally, at the third store we tried, she held one up. "This is it," she said, pushing me toward the dressing room. "Try it on."

The dress was red, and I have to say, it was really pretty. It had thin little straps over the shoulders and it wasn't so tight that it made me feel weird about my body. The skirt part ended just above my knees, and when I turned around, it twirled a little bit.

"I love it," I told my mother.

"Now for the next part of the plan," she said mysteriously.

After we paid for the dress, she took me by the hand and led me out of the store. "Where are we going?" I asked her. "I've got my dress."

"You can't wear a dress like that with hair like that," she said, leading me into a salon.

I started to protest, but she ignored me. Instead, she spoke to the man behind the salon's desk for a minute. I saw him look over at me a couple of times and nod his head. I had no idea what they were talking about, but I was suddenly very nervous.

My mother motioned for me to come over to them. "This is Carl," she said. "I'm going to leave you with him. I'll be back later."

"What's he going to do?" I asked her.

"Don't worry," Carl said. "You're going to be beautiful."

My mother left, and Carl had me sit in a chair. He took the band off of my ponytail and my hair fell around my shoulders. I was surprised at how long it had gotten.

"All right," Carl said, walking around me. "I think I know just what to do. Are you ready to be transformed?"

"I guess so," I said doubtfully.

Carl proceeded to wash my hair. Then he brought out a tub of some funny-colored gel and started to apply it to my hair. I didn't know if it was conditioner or what, and I didn't ask. To tell the truth, I was afraid to find out. I was especially afraid when Carl put these squares of silver paper around parts of my hair and folded them up like wontons.

"Now let's see what we can do about those arms," Carl said.

I'd forgotten about my blue arms. I guess I'd gotten used to them. Now that Carl had reminded me, I looked at them and felt awful all over again. They were going to look so stupid with my red dress, like I was a walking American flag.

"What can you do?" I asked Carl.

He smiled. "Magic," he said. "Just wait."

He disappeared, returning with another tub of goo. This time, he took a brush and brushed the stuff onto my arms and hands. It tingled a little, but it didn't hurt or anything. When the blue parts of my arms were all covered, he put the tub down.

"Ten minutes," he said. "I'll be back."

He left me alone to tingle. It felt like the longest ten minutes of my life. I kept looking down at my arms. The goo was turning a funny color, sort of orangey, and I was afraid it was doing something weird to my skin. I looked around for help, but everybody was busy, and I was afraid to interrupt them. So I just sat there, watching my arms turn orange and trying not to worry.

Finally, Carl came back. He had me stick my arms in the sink, where he rinsed them with warm water. As the orange goo slid off, I was surprised to see my normal skin underneath.

"See?" Carl said. "I told you. Magic."

"What is it?" I asked him.

"Bleaching cream," he answered. "What do you think of the results?"

I held up my hand. There was no trace of the dye. "I think it's fantastic," I said, so happy I almost started to cry.

"We usually use it on women cursed with unfortunate moustaches," said Carl. "But we also use it to get dye off when we get it on our hands. I thought it might work, and thank goodness it did. Now let's get back to your hair."

He turned me around and put the chair back so that my head was in the sink. I felt him removing the foil squares, and then water was running over my head. While he rinsed my hair, I kept looking at my hands. I still couldn't believe that I was back to normal. I couldn't wait to show my mother.

Carl wrapped a towel around my hair and had me walk over to another chair. When I sat down, he turned me around so that I was looking at myself in a mirror. Then he undid the towel and pulled it away.

I gasped. My hair was its normal reddish-brown color, but with lighter highlights here and there. It wasn't a huge change, but it made me look totally different.

"Like it?" Carl asked.

I couldn't speak. All I could do was reach up and touch my hair. I kept touching it, afraid it was fake and would come off if I pulled on it too hard.

"I'll take that as a yes," said Carl, picking up a pair of scissors. "Now sit back and relax."

He began cutting my hair, taking off little pieces here and there. I watched the bits fall to the floor, where they started to make a pretty big pile. I was sort of afraid he was cutting too much off, but he seemed to know what he was doing, so I let him do it.

When he was done, he turned me around again so that I couldn't see myself. Then he dried my hair, brushing it and teasing it. Finally, he turned the blow dryer off and put it down.

"Finished," he said. "Ready to see it?"

I nodded. Carl spun the chair around, and I saw myself in the mirror. My hair was beautiful. Carl had cut it to just above my shoulders, which I never would have thought would work on me, but it totally did. I had bangs, and the whole thing looked amazing.

"I'm pretty," I said softly. "I'm really pretty." I looked at Carl. "Thank you so much," I said.

He put his hand on my shoulder. "It was all there already," he said. "I just brought it out."

I thought we were done, but Carl had more surprises for me. He took me over to another part of the salon, where a woman did my nails. She filed and buffed them, then applied a coat of clear polish. I couldn't believe my short, sensible nails could ever look nice, but somehow, they did.

And I *still* wasn't finished. After the nails, I went to yet another table. This time, a man showed me how to put on makeup. Not a lot, but enough so that my face looked more alive. And all it took was some blush and tinted lip gloss. The man had me do it myself, so that I knew I could do it again any time I wanted to.

By the time my mother came back for me, I was a different person. When she saw me, her mouth fell open, and I thought she might cry.

"I know," I said, hugging her. "It's a new me."

"No," she said, sounding like Carl. "It's the same you. Just cleaned up a little." Now that two people had said it, I was almost starting to believe it myself.

"Thank you," I said. "For everything."

"You're very welcome," she said. Then she looked at her watch. "We have to go. We need to be at the club in an hour."

We left the mall and hurried home. There I put on my dress, along with some shoes my mother had picked up while I was getting my makeover. When I was all ready, I stood in front of the mirror and looked at myself. Carl and my mom were right; I was still Allie. But I looked fantastic.

"Who's the ugly stepsister now?" I said to the mirror.

Chapter Nineteen

The party had already started when we arrived at the country club. Families had spread out blankets on the grass and were enjoying picnic lunches. Some of the younger kids were already running around with sparklers in their hands, even though it was only about two o'clock and you could barely see the tiny stars shooting from them.

Then there were the dogs. A lot of people had brought their dogs with them, and they were running around on the grass having a great time. I saw some of the older club members eyeing them suspiciously. Probably, I thought, they were afraid the dogs would dig up the lawn or do their business right on a rose bush or something. But as far as I could see, the dogs were behaving just fine.

We'd brought Rufus with us, of course. He had on a brand-new red collar that matched my dress perfectly. Some of the other dogs had more elaborate costumes. I saw dogs with flag bandanas tied around their necks, dogs with hats, and even one dog dressed like the Statue of Liberty. Mostly, though, the dogs didn't have anything on, which I was happy to see. It looked like most people agreed with me that dogs didn't need to be dressed up.

For once I couldn't wait to run into Megan. I wanted her to see how great I looked. And I didn't have to wait long. Not five minutes after I walked outside, I heard her voice behind me.

"I can't believe it," she said.

She sounded completely shocked, which made me happy. Her reaction was even better than I'd hoped it would be. Fixing a huge smile on my face, I turned around, ready to enjoy my big moment. But when I saw Megan, my smile disappeared.

"You copied my dress!" she said.

It was true. Not the copying part—I had no idea what she was going to wear to the party—but the part about our dresses being the same. Exactly the same. Well, except for the fact that Megan had a corsage of red, white, and blue roses pinned to hers. I stared at Megan and she stared back. She was so mad, she didn't even notice my hair, my nails, or my arms. All she could see was the dress. *Her* dress. And all I could see was the corsage.

Even if I hadn't heard her hinting to Jack about the corsage, I would have known he got it for her, because he was standing next to her. He was staring at me, too, as if he couldn't believe I would copy Megan. His eyes were wide, and his mouth was sort of hanging open.

"Oooh," Megan said, stamping her foot. "I should have known you'd try to ruin this for me.

You ruin *everything*. Why can't you just disappear?" She grabbed Jack's hand. "Come on," she said. "I can't stand to look at her."

Jack hesitated, like he wanted to say something to me. But he wasn't there with me; he was there with Megan. The two of them walked off together.

I stood there, alone, not knowing what to do. I didn't have another dress to change into. Besides, I liked the one I had on. It wasn't my fault that stupid Megan had picked out the same one. Like everything lately, it was just another accident.

All I could do was walk around the party, watching other people have a good time while I got more and more upset. All around me, people were laughing and enjoying themselves. But I just felt defeated. No matter what I did, it turned out wrong. I was, I felt certain, destined to be a loser girl forever. Shan would run off with Hector and then I'd have no one. It would just be me and Rufus.

Speaking of Rufus, he had disappeared. I

decided to go looking for him, afraid he might have gone after a squirrel or something. The last thing I needed was another Regrettable Incident to deal with.

I found him by the pond, which didn't surprise me. Labs love water, and he'd gone right to it. There were a couple of other dogs there with him, and they were splashing around in the shallow water. Out on the pond, about a dozen rowboats were floating lazily. Each one had a couple in it. I watched them having fun, rowing around in circles while I stood on the shore, alone.

In one of the boats, Megan and Jack sat with Tallulah and Barkley. Megan was holding Tallulah, who was still blue, on her lap while Barkley hung his nose over the side, looking at the water. I could see that Megan had dressed Tallulah in some stupid outfit. She had apparently gotten over our dress disaster, because she was talking a mile a minute, waving at some of the Megbots who were in other boats with their dates.

"I can't believe he's here with her," I said.

And I couldn't. For the life of me, I didn't understand what Jack was doing with Megan. It just made no sense. But it didn't really matter anymore. He *was* there with her, and I was all by myself.

I heard a whoosh as someone behind me let off a bottle rocket. I saw it whiz up over the pond and explode in a shower of sparks. Barking excitedly, some of the dogs started running around. Then another bottle rocket went off, and another. A series of explosions popped and whistled as they sailed over the pond.

I heard a dog start yapping loudly. I thought it sounded familiar, and looked around to see where it was coming from. Out on the pond, I spied Tallulah jumping up and down in the rowboat. Megan was trying to catch her, but she was too worked up. She was running hysterically from one end of the boat to the other.

Then she jumped over the side. I watched as Megan stood up, trying to catch her. It was too late, though. Tallulah was already in the water, splashing her paws frantically as she tried to swim. Megan leaned over, trying to reach her, and that's when the whole boat turned sideways.

It seemed to hang there for a second. Then I heard Megan shriek, and the boat turned over. Megan, Jack, and Barkley were dumped into the pond along with Tallulah. I saw Megan's head disappear under the water, then bob back up. She was screaming and thrashing around.

Jack swam over to her and tried to calm her down. Barkley, being a spaniel, simply swam for shore, his body moving smoothly and calmly through the water. But I couldn't see Tallulah. She had disappeared. I knew she couldn't have made it to shore already, so I searched the pond for her.

I finally spotted her, about fifty feet from shore. Only her nose was above the water. She was struggling. It looked like her paws had gotten stuck in her costume. She was sinking, and unless someone got to her soon, she was going to drown. The people in the boats were too busy watching Megan to notice her.

"Her dog!" I shouted. "Help her dog!"

Three of the Megbots turned and looked at me. I pointed to Tallulah, who was quickly sinking. They just stared, doing nothing. I couldn't believe it!

Someone had to do something or Tallulah was going to drown. I looked around, but nobody was going to help her. *You have to do it*, I told myself.

Trying not to think about my dress, I slipped off my shoes and ran into the water. It was cold, but I ignored that and started swimming. I kicked as hard as I could, heading for Tallulah. I hoped I could get to her in time.

I reached her just as she was going under. Just as I'd thought, her little feet were all wrapped up in the stupid striped sweater Megan had put on her. She was whimpering, and for the first time ever, I felt sorry for her.

"It's okay," I said as I pulled her to my chest and held her. "It's okay, sweetie. You're safe now."

Tallulah pressed against me, shivering, as I

swam with her back to shore. A crowd had gathered to watch what was going on, and when I walked out of the pond, water dripping from my dress and my hair plastered flat against my head, everyone clapped. Even the dogs barked, like they knew I had helped one of them.

I pulled the sweater off of Tallulah. Someone handed me a towel and I wrapped her in it, drying her little body while she continued to shake. Slowly, as she realized she wasn't in the water anymore, she settled down.

My mother came over and wrapped a second towel around me. "Are you all right?" she asked.

"I'm fine," I said. "I think the dress has had it, though."

"You can always get another dress," said my mother. She looked at Tallulah. "You can't replace her."

"No, you can't," I said, looking at the little blue dog. "She's definitely one of a kind."

"Look at my dress!" I heard Megan's voice. She was coming out of the water. Jack was behind her, but she ignored him. She was trying to wring the water out of her dress. She didn't even notice that I was holding Tallulah until Jack pointed to us. Then all Megan did was come over, snatch Tallulah out of my arms, and flounce off.

"You're welcome," I said as my mother shook her head.

Jack looked at me, then at Megan's retreating back. "That was a cool thing you did," he said to me.

All of a sudden I felt cold. My dress was clinging to my body, and it felt clammy and awful. Even though it was warm out, I was shivering. I wished Jack would hold me and make me feel warmer, the same way I had Tallulah. I even thought he might.

Then my mother said, "We need to get you out of that wet dress."

Leaving Jack, we walked up to the clubhouse. I hadn't brought any other clothes with me, but my mother found a T-shirt and some shorts in the lost and found box, and I put those on. They looked ridiculous on me, but at least I was dry again.

"How's it feel to be a hero?" my father asked when I came back outside.

"Wet," I said. He laughed. Then he put his arm around me and hugged me. "I'm proud of you," he said.

That warmed me up even more. But I was still depressed. It felt good to have saved Tallulah, but my makeover was ruined. Megan was still a jerk, and Jack was, well, I didn't know what Jack was.

"Can we go home?" I asked my parents.

My father looked at me. "You'll miss the fireworks," he said.

I groaned. "I think I've had enough fireworks for one day," I told him.

Chapter Twenty

When we got home, the first thing I did was take a hot bath. A long one. I even filled the tub with bubbles, and when the water cooled down, I let it out and filled it again. *That's* how depressed I was.

Wait. It gets worse. After the bath, I ate almost an entire pint of mint chocolate chip ice cream. By myself. Alone in my room, finishing *Pride & Prejudice*. And I cried through the whole last chapter, snuffling into my ice cream and wishing my life could end as happily as Elizabeth's and Darcy's.

I know that earlier I said that when I'm depressed I take Rufus for a walk and it cheers me up. Well, apparently sometimes you *do* need to just wallow around in self-pity. If Shan had been there, I know she would have joined me for the ice cream. And we would have talked about how boys suck and mean girls suck and being the girl that bad things always happen to sucks.

But Shan wasn't there. She was at a Fourth of July picnic with Hector, which I knew because I'd tried calling her and got her grandfather again. *I bet she's already kissed him,* I thought. Great.

Okay, I'll be the first to admit that being alone on the Fourth of July is hardly the same as being alone on, say, Valentine's Day. But it was still a downer. Big-time. Because the thing was, I should have been having a great time. I should have been watching fireworks, in my beautiful dress, with Jack McKenna sitting next to me thinking how great I looked and how he really, really wanted to lean over and kiss me. And then, right when the biggest, brightest, most sparkly fireworks exploded right over our heads, he *would* kiss me.

Instead I was sitting at home, feeling bloated from eating so much ice cream and thinking about the *two* dresses I'd managed to ruin. And when Shan called later to tell me that she and Hector *had* kissed, I would have to pretend to be happy for her instead of getting to tell her that Jack and I had kissed too and comparing our first real kisses. Well, I just wouldn't answer the phone.

I went to bed as soon as it was dark enough to count as nighttime. When I woke up the next morning, I could tell I was getting a cold. I felt a little feverish, and my nose was stuffed up. *Great,* I thought. *Now I get to be sick on top of everything else.* I rolled over, pulled the blankets around me, and tried to go back to sleep. But I couldn't, so I got up and went downstairs to scrounge up some breakfast.

My father had already gone to work, but my mother was frying bacon at the stove. Rufus was sitting right next to her, hoping she might drop a piece. I flopped down in a chair and put my head on the table. "I don't feel so good," I said. "I mean well," I corrected myself, thinking of Shan. "I don't feel so well."

"You probably caught a chill from being in the water," my mother said, setting a plate of scrambled eggs and bacon in front of me. "Eat. It will make you feel better."

I picked up a piece of bacon and bit into it. Normally I'm not a big fan of eating animals, but sometimes I can't help myself. I know that's not an excuse or anything, but give me a break. Sometimes a girl needs her bacon.

I finished the bacon and poked at the eggs. Those I wasn't so excited about. But I put some ketchup on them and they weren't too bad. And my mom was right; I did feel better once I'd eaten something. I could still feel the cold trying to creep up on me, but it didn't seem quite so bad.

"I think I'm going to take Rufus for a walk," I said.

"If you can get him away from the bacon," said my mother.

I went and put on my sneakers, but left on

the sweatpants and T-shirt I'd worn to bed. I was just going out for a walk, not a date, and Ruf didn't care what I wore. He was just happy to be going out.

Rufus pulled me down the sidewalk toward the park. "No, boy," I said, making him stop. "I was thinking more like around the block. Maybe two blocks."

Rufus whined. He looked at me with his big, sad eyes and wagged his tail. I sighed. "Fine," I said. "We'll go to the park."

He practically dragged me there, he was so excited. I trotted along behind him, glad that I'd worn my sneakers. When we reached the park, I looked around to make sure there was nobody for Rufus to bother, then let him off his leash. Almost immediately, he took off. I saw a fluffy tail streaking away in front of him. *I should have seen that coming,* I thought as Rufus and the squirrel disappeared in the direction of the Dog Bowl.

I ran after him. When I reached the Bowl, I looked down and saw him playing with a familiar black-and-white dog. It was Barkley. And if Barkley was there, that meant that . . .

"Hi," Jack said, making me jump. He was standing behind me.

"Hi," I muttered, trying not to look at him.

"Isn't this how we met?" he said, looking at Rufus and Barkley playing together.

"I'm surprised you remember," I said. "You certainly didn't remember me when you saw me at the shelter." I was suddenly very much aware that I was wearing old sweatpants, and found myself pushing my hair behind my ears.

"You mean when you came to pick up your *best friend's* dog," Jack said.

I felt my cheeks burn. "So I didn't exactly tell the truth," I said. "You didn't have to rat on me to Megan."

"What?" said Jack, looking confused.

I turned on him. "Come on," I said. "I know you called Megan that day and told her Tallulah was there. How else would she have found out?"

Jack shook his head. "You think I would do that?" he asked.

"Well, didn't you?" I demanded.

"No," he answered. "Tallulah has a micro-chip."

I looked at him, not understanding.

"A Home Again microchip," Jack repeated. "The kind you put in dogs in case they get lost. The chip has the owner's information on it. We put them in every dog that gets adopted from the shelter."

I did know about the chips. Rufus had one. It was really small, about the size of a grain of rice. It was injected under the skin, and anyone with a special scanner could read it if they had to. It was a great way to help lost animals find their owners. It hadn't occurred to me that Tallulah might have one.

"Tallulah's a registered show dog, even though they don't show her," Jack continued. "She's got a microchip. One of the volunteers ran the scanner on her, found the chip, and called Megan before you even came in. I didn't know, which is why I let you take her. For your information, *I'm* the one who got in big trouble for letting you have her."

I didn't know what to say. If Jack was telling the truth, I had made a horrible mistake. If he wasn't, then he was an even bigger jerkboy than I'd thought. Either way, it was bad for me.

"And by the way, I *did* recognize you when you came in. I just didn't want you to know."

"What?" I said. I hadn't really been paying attention. I was too busy trying to decide if he was a liar or not.

"I did recognize you," Jack repeated. He sounded mad. "You know, I thought you were different. When I saw how you were with Rufus, I thought you were a girl I could really like. I can usually tell how people are by how they are with their dogs. But I guess I read you wrong."

I just stared at him. He'd just said basically the same thing I'd been thinking about him. I'd liked him right away not just because he was cute, but because he had such a sweet dog. Had I been right after all?

"But Megan . . ." I said.

"What about Megan?" Jack asked. He had pulled Barkley's leash from the belt loop of his jeans and looked like he was about to leave.

"You like her," I said.

He shook his head so that the hair flipped away from his eyes. "Like her?" he said as he waved for Barkley to come to him. "I can barely stand her. All she does is talk about herself, and those friends of hers are so boring I have to tune them out when they start talking."

"But you took her to Magic Mountain," I said. "And the Fourth of July party. You bought her a corsage."

Jack held up a finger. "Correction," he said. "I didn't *take* her anywhere. I *went* with her. And I only did that because my parents made me."

"Made you?" I said. "Why would they make you hang out with Megan?"

"Because my mother works with her father," said Jack, snapping the leash on Barkley's collar. "She's a lawyer at his firm. She thought it would look good if I was nice to his daughter."

Suddenly, everything made sense. I couldn't believe I hadn't seen it before. Of course Jack's parents would want him to be nice to Megan. That *totally* explained why he'd put up with her. But I'd been so angry, and so focused on how much Megan bugged me, that I hadn't seen the truth. Now that I did, I was afraid it was too late.

"I've got to go," said Jack, starting to walk down the hill.

"Wait," I called after him, fumbling as I tried to attach Rufus's leash.

He turned and looked at me. But I didn't know what to say. Everything was all mixed up. My feelings were bouncing all over the place and my stomach was in knots. I stared at Jack. In the sun, his eyes sparkled brown and gold. And that's when I realized: He *was* my prince. Only he wasn't about to kiss me, he was about to leave.

Then you need to kiss him, said the voice in my head. You know, the one that had gotten me into so much trouble already. I didn't know — should I listen to it one more time? Or was I about to have the biggest Regrettable Incident of my life? I mean, in fairy tales the prince always does the kissing. The princess is just supposed to wait for him.

Maybe it's time to rewrite those stories, I thought.

I ran toward Jack. Only I guess Rufus thought we were playing a game. He ran so quickly that I was pulled along behind him. Instead of stopping in front of Jack, I sort of ran *into* him. But he caught me. His hands were on my arms, and I was looking into his face. For what seemed like forever, I stared into his eyes. What was I doing? I wondered. I was wearing sweats. My hair was a mess. I had a cold. If I could possibly look worse, I didn't know how. But I wanted to tell him how I felt, and if I was going to do that, I had to do it now.

"You weren't wrong," I said. "*I* was. And I'm sorry."

Jack didn't say anything. He just looked back at me. I knew he was thinking about how crazy I was. I was about to tell him not to listen to me, that I was on cold medication and completely out of my mind. I started to pull away, but he pulled me back.

"Remember when I told you at the club that

I wanted to ask you something?" he said.

I nodded, afraid to speak.

"I wanted to ask you if you would go out with me. On a date."

"A date?" I said.

"Yeah," he said. "A date. I like you, Allie. You're a little weird sometimes, but so am I. Besides, Barkley likes you, and that's a pretty good recommendation." Then he started blushing. "I liked you the first time I saw you. And no, it wasn't just because you're beautiful."

I started to say something. Then I realized what he'd just said. He thought I was beautiful? All along? I couldn't believe it!

"A date," I said when I was able to form an actual sentence. "With you."

He nodded.

"I think I can do that," I said. My head was spinning. All I could see were Jack's eyes and the summer light on his hair. Everything else was fuzzy, like in a dream.

"There's something else I've wanted to do," said Jack.

That's when it happened. IT. The kiss. Jack

leaned down and his lips met mine. I forgot about my old sweats, my messy hair, Megan, where to put my nose, when to breathe, everything. I felt Jack's arms go around me, and I put mine around him. I don't know how long the kiss lasted. Maybe only a few seconds. Maybe an hour. It didn't matter. It was perfect.

Jack pulled his head back and looked at me. He ran his tongue over his lips. "You taste like bacon," he said.

Okay, so it wasn't *all* like it is in the movies. But life usually isn't. Besides, this was better. Jack and I laughed. Then he kissed me again. As we kissed, Rufus barked. I looked down. He and Barkley were wagging their tails.

Remember when I made that wish on the Dog Star? I never said what I wished for. Well, now I can, because standing there with Jack, my wish came true.

Ready for your next first kiss?
Here's an excerpt from
It Had to Be You
by Sabrina Jordan

I went back to the counter. "Could I exchange this cone for one with rainbow sprinkles?"

"Yeah, right," the guy laughed, not bothering to look up from the skateboarding magazine he was flipping through. "Ice cream is nonreturnable."

Wise guy!

Before ordering another cone, I double-checked with Tommy to make sure I was getting *exactly* what he wanted—that there was no sugar cone versus wafer cone rule that I was unaware of.

"Thank you," he said, taking a bite out of his cone after I'd handed it to him.

Finally I'd done something right in his eyes!

Now what was I going to do with this other cone? I hated chocolate ice cream but I didn't want to throw the cone out. Then I saw Aaron in the bowling alley's video arcade with Michael. Luckily, Aaron will eat anything.

"Aaron!" I called out. "Aaron!"

My brother came over to our lane. "What do you want?" he asked.

I offered my brother the ice-cream cone.

"What's wrong with it?" he asked suspiciously.

"There's nothing wrong with it," I huffed, shoving it into his hand. "Tommy doesn't like chocolate sprinkles."

"Who's Tommy?" he asked, opening his mouth wide and inhaling half the cone in one bite, which caused Tommy's mouth to drop open. And promptly want to try the same thing with his cone. Of course, his cone couldn't fit into his tiny mouth, and a second later his entire lower face was smeared with vanilla and chocolate ice cream and sprinkles.

I pointed to Tommy and Megan as I began cleaning Tommy's face with a napkin. Naturally he started squirming like an eel and wouldn't stand still. "Our new next-door neighbors.

2

I'm babysitting them tonight for their older brother, Kyle."

"Aren't you going to throw a ball, Emma?" Megan asked.

I will be the first to admit that I'm not the world's best bowler. No matter how hard I try, the ball never goes where I want it to. If I throw it to the left, it goes to the right. If I throw it to the right, it goes to the left. If I try to throw a straight ball, it curves. Whenever I bowl, my score is pathetically low, as opposed to my brothers, who are always breaking 200. I'm lucky if my score breaks 100.

"I can give you some pointers if you want," Aaron offered.

"Thanks, but we're just messing around."

Aaron shrugged. "Suit yourself," he said, before going back to Michael.

Megan and I played two games. (I bowled a 90 and a 75 compared to Megan's 50 and 73.) We had just started our third game when Kyle arrived at the alley.

"Kyle!" Tommy and Megan exclaimed

happily, running to give him a hug.

Watching Tommy and Megan hug their older brother, I wondered what it would be like to hug him.

Wait a second!

Where had *that* thought suddenly come from?

Well, Kyle certainly *was* huggable. There was no denying that.

And ever since Kyle had moved next door, I found myself thinking of him more and more.

Before I could give it some extra thought, though, Kyle said, "I saw the way you throw your ball."

"And?" I put a hand on my hip and gave him a challenging look. "Think you can do any better?"

"I think I can."

Kyle found a ball that fit. Then he threw it down the alley and got a strike, sending all the pins flying, which caused Tommy to start hooting and hollering. I'd somehow gotten a strike the last game but Tommy hadn't applauded my efforts. Hmph!

"Anyone can become a better bowler," Kyle said. "It's just a matter of concentration. See those arrows on the lane?"

"What arrows?"

"Those," Kyle said, pointing them out to me.

"Are they important?"

Kyle stood behind me and slipped my fingers into my ball. Then he lifted my arm up and back in a straight line. "You need to keep your arm straight when you throw your ball. You twist your wrist, which is why your straight ball is never straight. Also, and this is very important, if you focus on a particular arrow when you throw the ball, the ball will go where you want after you release it."

I tried to pay attention to everything Kyle was telling me but I was unable to.

The only thing I was able to focus on was having Kyle so close!

He smelled like soap and summer and coconut and cologne all wrapped up together.

Like most of my friends, I hadn't really started dating yet. But I was definitely wondering what it would be like to have a boyfriend now. I did have some crushes in junior high but that was *junior high*! Guys in junior high are *so* immature. They're more concerned about watching TV and playing video games. But Kyle was different. He seemed older. More confident. Thoughtful, as evidenced by the dinner he'd made for his parents.

And Tommy and Megan both adored him.

Keeping his instructions in mind, I focused on the arrows, concentrating on the one in the middle, and held my arm straight as I released my ball.

It went exactly where I wanted it to.

And I got a strike!

"Yay!" Megan shouted, jumping up and down. "Emma got a strike! Emma got a strike!"

"Your tips really worked!" I exclaimed, giving Kyle a hug, which was the last thing I expected to do.

But once I was into the hug, I went with it.

Other than hugging my dad and my brothers, I'd never really held a guy so close. This was different. I was aware of the hard muscles under his T-shirt as I wrapped my arms around him, pulling him close. And I liked how soft his skin felt as I pulled away after the hug ended, trailing my fingers down his arms.

I liked it a lot.

And I especially liked the fact that while I hugged Kyle, he hugged me back!

I couldn't really enjoy the moment, though, because just then the Gruesome Twosome arrived, otherwise known as my brothers Aaron and Michael.

"Who's the boy, Em?" Michael asked.

"That's the new guy, Kyle, from next door," Aaron explained. "Hey, Emma, why are you letting *him* give you bowling tips? I offered to help her before but she didn't want my help. Do you *like* Kyle or something?" Aaron began batting his eyelashes and making kissing noises, trying to imitate my voice. "Kiss me, Kyle! Kiss me!"

"KYLE DOESN'T WANT TO KISS EMMA!" Tommy shouted. "SHE'S ICKY!"

I. Was. Going. To. Kill. My. Brothers.

A quick glimpse at Kyle showed that he was blushing red.

I raced over to Aaron and Michael. "Get. Out. Of. Here. Now!" I growled between gritted teeth.

"She must really like this guy," Aaron said.

Michael grabbed Aaron by the arm. "Come on, let's leave her with her *boyfriend*."

"Bye, Kyle!" Aaron called out in his girly voice, waving good-bye.

Once I saw my brothers walk out of the bowling alley, I turned back to Kyle, who was no longer blushing. Had he heard what Aaron said? About me liking him? I hoped not. Because I *did* like him but not *like* him *like* him. The way you did a boyfriend. I liked him as a friend.

Didn't I?